AN AERO ISLAND CHRISTMAS MYSTERY

ADRIANA LICIO

The Home Travellers
Press

AN AERO ISLAND CHRISTMAS MYSTERY
A Danish Cozy Mystery

Book 3 in the ***The Homeswappers*** series
By Adriana Licio

Edition I

Cover by **Wicked Smart Design**
Editing by **Alison Jack**

To all of us dreamers,
Who long for an island
Where people live in peace.

CONTENTS

1

CROSSING THE BALTIC

It was a glorious, if chilly day. The sky was a perfect Copenhagen blue, the sun was shining, the Svendborg harbour looked increasingly cosy and small as the ferry left the mainland to cross the Baltic sea. Short stretches of land – you could barely call them islands – were scattered around, showing all shades of brown and green, and every colour in between.

But Concetta Natale Passolina, or simply Etta to her friends, was sitting stubbornly inside the ferry, determined to make her life as bleak as possible while the other passengers cried out enthusiastically on deck, taking photos or holding cups of coffee in their hands to warm them against the Northerly breeze.

A few minutes earlier, a member of the ferry staff had knocked on the window of a yolk-yellow Fiat 500 to announce to Etta that passengers were not allowed to stay in their cars during the 75-minute crossing and she should walk upstairs without further ado. The news had come as a great relief to two other passengers, who had felt obliged to keep her company, in the process distressing her even further.

Now sitting in a padded chair in the middle of the ferry's lounge, Etta wondered what she was doing so far north at the end of November, when it was excruciatingly cold. She and her two travelling companions had spent the first five days of their Danish stay in Copenhagen where it was already dark around four o'clock and the days were still getting shorter. The people in Denmark's capital hadn't made a great impression on her, despite what Dora, her dear friend, and lately housemate and travelling companion, too, had said about *hygge* – an untranslatable word that indicated a skill to create a diffuse state of cosiness and wellbeing around one's life – and despite her claims that the Danish were the happiest people on earth. Etta had found them austere, rushing around just as people did in any other big city, no one inclined to talk. In brief, they'd seemed as unhappy and miserable as everyone else in the world.

And now, here she was wondering how this home swap on the little island of Ærø, suspended in the Baltic between Denmark and Germany, would end up. It had been all very fine agreeing to the swap in the glorious summer; when the proposal had reached them via email, the pictures of the island showed fields of blond corn, pastel-coloured timbered houses with gorgeous hollyhocks growing next to brightly painted doors. Now they were here in the cold and dark of a bleak Nordic winter.

Obviously, that morning, the whole world was actively determined to trouble her. A tall, straight-faced woman about Etta's age, carrying a multitude of bags of all sizes, sat next to her.

"No other place around to sit, is there?" Etta asked, looking at the ferry's almost empty interior. There were plenty of comfy chairs next to the windows. The woman shrugged. Maybe she didn't speak English, which was rather unusual as so far, all the people Etta and Dora had met in Copenhagen seemed to speak better English than many Brits themselves.

The woman spread her luggage beneath the seat, up in the racks, on a trolley next to her, a smaller bag between her legs. In doing so, she knocked her knee against Etta's, invading the feisty Italian woman's space.

"And what about Northerners and their celebrated reserved manners?" she snapped.

"If you have a problem with me sitting next to you, you're free to move wherever you please," the woman replied in good English, pointing to the rest of the boat.

"Why should I move somewhere else when I was here first?"

"Because this is my seat."

"Your seat?" Etta asked, bewildered. "I didn't see any reservation signs."

"You dumbo! Don't you know that tourists always want to sit close to the windows to shoot pictures and inundate all their relatives and friends with the stupidest selfies ever? So I sit here, knowing no one will disturb me."

"Well, it looks like it's not your lucky day." Etta grinned, suddenly satisfied. If there was anything that could make her life happier on a cold winter's day, it was making someone else's life miserable.

The woman opened one of her bags to extract a book and started reading, placing her elbow on the common armrest. Immediately, Etta was annoyed again, resenting this second attack on her private space. Pretending a big, elongated yawn, she pushed her elbow against her neighbour's. The woman started; her book fell on the bag between her legs.

"Oh, I'm *so* sorry," said Etta insincerely, "but these chairs are too small, it's easy to invade one another's space without realising it."

"I guess it can be quite difficult for ageing women to control their movements."

"You must know as you've clearly been ageing for the last twenty years!"

The two women's voices had been rising sharply throughout this altercation and a member of staff came over to them.

"Sille, is there anything wrong?" the stewardess asked Etta's sparring partner.

"Just one tourist too many."

The young woman smiled at her. "You know we depend on tourists to keep the island alive, so please, why don't you come over and sit next to me? I have been reading an antiques magazine and I was just wondering if you could give me your opinion on a couple of items featured in it."

The older woman replied in Danish, almost certainly a joke at Etta's expense. The stewardess couldn't help chuckling, then she helped Etta's unwelcome neighbour to move her luggage elsewhere. As they left, the stewardess flashed a smile at Etta, winking at her.

Etta sighed as loudly as she could, marking her victory over her adversary.

"Sod off, Maddalena," she grumbled, addressing her daughter, who at that moment would be in her home in Granada, as if the younger woman were there beside her. "Do as you please for Christmas, I don't care. I've got plenty of ammunition to enjoy myself any way I can." And she put her elbows on both armrests and breathed in deeply to savour her victory better.

ON THE DECK, DOROTEA ROSA PEPE, OR SIMPLY DORA to her friends, was inhaling the chilly air in small gulps as if she was tasting it. It was sharp and salty, and so different from the Mediterranean breeze, she found it exhilarating as it filled her lungs. And then there was the amazing view. Svendborg harbour was falling behind and a scattering of islands were appearing all around, some barren, others featuring cute little houses. A few trees here, a jetty on the seafront there offered a completely new perspective to her curious and generally romantic mind.

She was so enraptured by the beauty of it all that she had clasped her hands, letting go of the leash she should have been holding. By the time Dora woke up from her daydreams, the leash was nowhere to be seen. And neither was the dog who was attached to it.

"Don't let Leon wander free!" Etta's dire warning echoed in Dora's head. "I don't dare to imagine how these Viking people will react if they're mad at someone for breaking their rules."

But it was too late.

NAPOLEON, OR SIMPLY LEON TO HIS FRIENDS, WAS A self-confident Basset Hound. The previous summer, he had allowed himself to be adopted by his two ladies following the unfortunate demise of his previous human, the Night Watchman of Leon's native town, Rothenburg ob der Tauber, and had followed them to the small village of Castelmezzano in Southern Italy, where the citizens had turned him into a local celebrity. But as much fun as being a superstar was, Leon and his two humans also enjoyed travelling Europe, using a thing the women called a home swap scheme. They talked of being pensioners and living on a budget, whatever that might mean. No matter. Leon's inquisitive mind appreciated the opportunity to see more of the big, wide world.

He'd never been on a ferry before, but he loved the fresh, energising air that sent his nostrils quivering as if he were in a field of rabbits and pheasants. The impulse to hunt had been so strong that when the sweet biped had clasped her hands in contemplation (the feisty biped was inside missing all the fun – humans could be so odd sometimes), he couldn't resist the temptation to have his own little tour.

With the leash click-clacking behind him, a red bandana with a white cross that his sweet biped had said was the Danish flag around his neck, he started to explore the boat, tail up, the white flock at the top whipping the air. People were looking at him and smiling, but he could not stop; he was on a mission. He had to understand where the excitement he felt was coming from.

He walked along the whole deck, up and down the stairs, stopping only to confront two dogs. Both were larger than him, but he soon taught them he was the boss, a fact highlighted by his being free to come and go as he pleased, while they were on a leash. He didn't so much as look at a small dog barking loudly at him. Making that sort of a fuss was a sure sign of weakness, not worthy of his attention, so he carried on with a studied indifference.

"Hey, what are you doing, young fellow?" a steward addressed him. "Where's your owner?"

That, of course, was the wrong question; Leon was not owned by anybody. On the contrary, he owned a couple of ladies: a stiff-necked cantankerous one, and a dreamy far-too-compassionate one. It was he who had to take great care that none of the three of them got into trouble, but even a dedicated self-denying Basset needed a break from work every now and then.

Ignoring the steward, Leon scampered up the stairs on his left, reaching the upper deck. Most people had gone inside as the air had turned colder, but in a corner were a couple of children. The older one was sitting on the deck, his legs spread out in front of him, completely immersed in reading a book; the smaller one was climbing the ship's railing.

Leon stiffened. *No,* he thought, *that isn't good at all.*

2

TO THE RESCUE!

Leon had no hesitation. He launched himself into a short sprint, passing through the legs of an adult who had their whole attention focused on taking photos of the view. Startled by the metallic clang of the leash's hook, even the reader raised his eyes from the book as Leon ran past him. The dog got hold of a flap of the child's skirt and pulled with all his might.

The child was so surprised that her hands let go of the railing and she found herself tumbling, her back and head falling against the Basset's body. She started to cry, more out of shock than pain, but Leon was unmoved by the baby tears.

"Woof, woof, WOOF!"

The photographer cried out to the steward who had been following Leon.

"That dog has attacked a child! Hopefully he hasn't bitten her too savagely."

The other child sprang on to his feet and was next to the sobbing girl in half a second, shortly followed by a man who had emerged from the ferry's bar, holding a cup of hot coffee.

"My goodness, Emma, did you hurt yourself?" the man asked, putting his coffee on the deck and hugging her.

"Yes," she cried. "Actually, no."

"Did the dog hurt her?" The steward was out of breath, more from anxiety than rushing over to join them.

"No, he pulled her back as she was climbing on the railing," the older child explained.

"Emma!" the man said, clutching the child's shoulders. "Did you really do such an idiotic thing?"

"I just wanted to look at the sea from somewhere high," the child sobbed.

"That was very stupid, but I was even more stupid for leaving you and going to get coffee."

The steward gave him a stern look. "You're lucky you have such a wise dog or we could have lost your daughter to the sea."

"She's been on the ferry time and time again, I've no idea what's got into her."

"All's well that ends well," the steward said. "But hopefully you've learned your lesson. By the time the ship had managed to stop, I doubt we would have had any chance of rescuing your child from the cold waters. If I were you, I'd serve this chap a special dinner tonight."

"I'd be honoured to do just that." The man hardly managed to speak, partly because his shock was choking him, partly because the child was clinging to him tightly. "The thing is, though, this is not our dog."

"He isn't?"

The man shook his head.

"But he can't have boarded all alone," said the steward.

"Certainly not."

"Leon!" Dora cried, panting. Although in her sixties, and a little on the rotund side to put it politely, she'd done a circuit of the whole ferry, running up and down the stairs, searching inside and out, only grateful that Etta had dozed off and hadn't caught sight of her as she sped through the lounge. "I hope you've done nothing too bad," she added, seeing a sobbing child, a concerned dad and a frowning steward.

"To tell you the truth, your dog has just saved my Emma from falling overboard," said the child's father. "I'm Flemming, nice to meet you."

"He ran like a bolt of lightning," the boy added, turning the hush pup into a super dog. "He seized her skirt and pulled her back to safety... By the way, I'm Thomas, Emma's brother."

"I guess I'd better get back to my job," the steward said, his voice still stern. "I hope no one else is thinking of attempting anything stupid today, and you, Emma, I hope you've learned your lesson."

"I'm sorry!" the little girl said with such compunction, the steward's heart melted and he had to turn away so as not to reveal the smile that was dawning on his face. As he left, Flemming had more to say to his daughter.

"And Emma, you'd better thank this lady, too. If she hadn't let the dog roam free..."

"Thanks a lot, Miss," Emma whispered in uncertain English, looking to her father for confirmation that she had chosen the right words. "I won't do that ever again."

"It's the most important thing," Dora smiled back, "that we learn from our mistakes. I believe you will never attempt anything as dangerous again."

Her father translated for Emma and the child looked at the tips of her feet, her two pigtails dancing up and down in the air as she nodded her complete agreement. The last two tears ran down her cheeks, almost meeting on her chin.

"My name's Dora and this young fellow is Napoleon, but you can call him Leon."

"Napoleon," the two children repeated, patting the dog and smiling. Flemming shook Dora's hand warmly.

"Will you be staying on the island for a few days?"

"Yes. In fact, we're swapping homes with a family from

Ærøskøbing. We've come to enjoy Christmas on the island. That is, we will stay for a couple of weeks leading up to Christmas and be back home before the day itself."

"We live in Ærøskøbing too," Thomas said, "so we can meet up and play with Leon... and you, too, of course."

"You've got to come to our house!" Emma cried. "Isn't that right, Dad?"

"Certainly," her father approved. "You and Leon are welcome guests anytime. How about dinner this evening?"

"We would be delighted, but tonight we're having dinner with our homeswap hosts..."

"Shouldn't they be staying at your house?"

"Not yet, they catch a flight from Copenhagen tomorrow. I guess we will have an early dinner, and then they will catch the last ferry tonight. They've booked a hotel close to Copenhagen airport."

"That's nice, you'll have a chance to get to know them." Flemming finally relaxed a little, sitting on a deckchair and inviting Dora to do likewise, the little one still cuddling up on his knee, looking all sweetness and innocence. "May I ask, who's the family you're swapping with? Don't think I'm nosy, we just know everyone on the island. We're such a small community."

"Certainly, you may. We're staying in the home of Freja and Magnus Holm. We can't wait to get to know them for real; so far, we've only exchanged emails and texts."

"They are very nice people and I'm sure you will love their house in the city centre. It's one of the old buildings... not that we have modern ones in Ærøskøbing. We islanders have always been so proud of our history and take great care to preserve our heritage at its best. But are you travelling all by yourself? I mean, just you and Leon?"

"Oh no, I'm travelling with a friend. She's taking a nap inside. And you, have you always lived on the island?"

"No, we used to live in Odense. That's where these two were

born. A few years back, you'd have found me stressed out in suit and tie."

"Well, we spent a few days in Copenhagen. For such a large city, it didn't seem as unfriendly and hectic as some can be," said Dora. As usual, she had got a very different impression to Etta.

"It might be that tourists get a different perspective, but for me, even the smaller Odense was too much. I am originally from the island of Ærø, as was my wife, and we used to come here for our holidays. We had always dreamed of our children growing up here."

"Your wife *was* from Ærø?" Dora repeated gently.

"A few years ago, after we moved to the island, she was diagnosed with leukaemia," the man said, his voice soft and resigned. "It was far too quick."

"Oh my goodness, I shouldn't have asked," Dora whispered, pointing to the two children.

"They know it all, and every week, they take her flowers…"

"And she looks down on us from up there," Emma said in Danish, looking to the cloudless sky, her father translating for her. "Only I don't understand why she doesn't visit, even once in a while."

"That's not true! She comes every night as soon as we close our eyes," Thomas said, his dark blue eyes seeming to get even darker and deeper.

"I'm sure she does," said Dora, Flemming again helping the children to understand what she was saying. "And she must be very proud of the two of you. Have you been on a little trip today?"

"We were visiting my sister and brother-in-law," replied Flemming. "They live close to Odense, and we're trying to convince them to move to the island…"

"So you're bringing up your children all by yourself?"

"There are good schools on the island and the children are

cared for until I finish work. Then we have the weekends to ourselves."

"And we have an excellent childminder, too," Thomas added with some pride.

"The good thing is," the man continued, "I'm a teacher at school, and thus our free time and holidays tend to coincide."

"Both my friend and I are retired teachers," cried Dora, surprised at the coincidence, as if teachers were a rare species.

As they went on chatting, Flemming asked Dora where she was from and told her that he and his wife had visited the South of Italy on a long backpacking tour before the children were born.

"We loved it there, such delicious food and welcoming people."

"We'll have to have you for dinner."

"But first, you've got to come to our place!" Thomas cried.

"I'd love you to come on Saturday," Flemming added.

"We'd love that, too." Dora beamed. They hadn't yet arrived on the island and had already received two invitations to dinner.

"That's Ærø!" Emma cried. Leon, thinking Ærø was some person or dog coming to challenge his authority, sprang up, startling the two children who had been patting him as he lay like a dead body.

"No, it's only the island," Thomas explained to him, pointing to the long green tongue of land. "And that's the Ærøskøbing harbour."

"My goodness," said Dora. "One whole hour has gone so quickly. I want to fetch Etta, my friend. She has to watch the arrival at least."

"We'll wait for you here," Flemming said.

"That would be nice." Taking Leon's leash, Dora started towards the stairs, then turned back to the family. "Please don't mention Leon running away from me... I'm so absent-minded, and Etta gets so cross..."

"We won't say a word about him wandering free," promised Flemming, smiling. "But we will say that Leon rescued Emma, we need to credit him for his bravery."

Again, Dora made a move, only to turn once more.

"I'm not sure how to put this," she said, blushing. "My friend, she might not be in the best of moods."

Flemming looked at her questioningly.

"You see, she received news from her daughter's family in Spain. They won't be coming to spend Christmas with us..."

"The poor thing, such a shame!"

"But don't tell her that you know, she doesn't like being pitied. So she might seem a little grumpy, but she's got a heart of gold."

"That's too much explanation, now." Flemming spoke with the resolution of someone used to the many whims of children. "We'll accompany you and say hello, she won't be able to resist two children and a dog asking her to come on the deck. Let's go."

Before they reached Etta, the little group passed close to where the young stewardess had sat the forthright woman called Sille who had invaded Etta's space. The children exchanged glances and shy greetings with her, but Flemming, suddenly brusque, told them to move on and ignored her.

When they reached Etta, to Dora's relief, she behaved civilly, though she frowned incredulously when Dora remarked how friendly the people from the island are. Thomas, in halting English, told Etta how Leon had broken free from Dora's leash at the sight of Emma climbing the railings on the side of the ferry. And Etta, despite herself, felt rather proud of her Basset and agreed to go outside to watch their arrival on Ærø.

~

Back in Dora's Fiat 500, Etta drove the ancient

little car out of the ferry's belly to the parking space at the port where their new home swapper friends would meet them. Flemming said he and the children would wait there too and introduce them to Freja and Magnus. The two children ran towards a young woman with long blonde hair tied back in a ponytail, a thick straight fringe almost covering her eyes, a smiley face with dimples and a lively air about her.

"Nathalie!" Emma cried, throwing herself into the young woman's arms. Nathalie kneeled down to hug the child and laughed as Emma's momentum threatened to knock her over. "We missed you so much!" Emma added as Nathalie lifted her into her arms.

"I missed you too. Loads." Nathalie hugged Thomas with her free arm, teasing him, "None of your friends is watching. How was it, Flemming?"

The man had seemed lost in thought, watching the interaction between his children and the young woman.

"Our stay was good," he replied finally. "And we met these two Italian ladies."

"So nice you should meet," Nathalie said, stretching out her hand and introducing herself. "I have come to pick you up as Freja is busy cooking and ordering Magnus about."

The two Italian friends shook hands with the young Danish woman.

"I'm Dora."

"And I'm Etta, and this is..."

"He can't be anyone but Leon, we're so glad to have him as a guest. And is that a Danish flag he's using as a bandana? He's gorgeous."

Leon accepted the cuddles and allowed himself to be laughed at; he wasn't at all indifferent to pretty ladies, both canine and human, and this one seemed to know how to handle a dog. She scratched below his ears and, more alarmingly, his bum, a most tender spot for a Basset. Being massaged right there sent waves of exhilaration throughout his body... surely she couldn't be allowed to excite him so publicly?

He tried to regain his composure, he had a reputation to defend. What if a pretty she-Basset passed by at that very moment?

"Is the house far from here?" Etta asked. She had done her share of driving across the long Danish bridges, then in and out of the ferry, a manoeuvre that alarmed her. What if a truck driver decided to squeeze their little Fiat? As a result, she felt she couldn't cope with any more driving challenges for the day.

"Just a few blocks ahead. Nothing is far on the island and Ærøskøbing is really a small town. I'm on my bike, you just have to follow me."

"Are you coming home, Nathalie? We have a lot of things to tell you," Thomas said. A cloud passed over Flemming's face.

"Pleeease," Emma added.

"I'm having dinner with these two ladies, then I'm accompanying Freja and Magnus to catch the last ferry so they can get on an early flight tomorrow. Can I come round and say goodnight to the children later tonight?" Nathalie asked Flemming.

"Only if they are in their pyjamas and ready for bed by 8.30, and no demanding bedtime stories."

"I promise, Dad."

"You have my word!"

"Such a lovely family," said Dora as Flemming and his children walked away with the promise that they would have dinner together on Saturday.

"They are indeed!" confirmed Nathalie.

"And I understand he's a widower," Dora remarked.

Nathalie flushed slightly. "And a stubborn widower, too. There's still a little light, let's move on. I'll take you through the Vestergade before turning towards the house so you can see what the town looks like. No spoiler intended, but it is charming."

"Are there any tiny alleys that are difficult to drive through?" asked Etta.

"Not really; the streets are ancient and cobbled, but easy to navigate. Please follow me."

3

DINNER WITH THE HOLMS

Dora spent most of her time in the car clasping her hands at the colourful half-timbered buildings. Generally one or two storeys with incredibly long curvy roofs and decorated wooden doors, they seemed more suited to elves than humans.

Nathalie stopped her bike and showed Etta where she could park the car, then they stood by the main door of one of the few three-storey buildings.

"I live above you on the first floor with my flatmate who's away for a couple of weeks," Nathalie explained as she helped Etta and Dora to drag the luggage down from the car roof box. "Once Freja and Magnus have gone, you can call on me anytime if you need help or a chat."

As they were standing on the pavement, Etta saw a shadow materialise at the window beside the main door. Nathalie opened the wooden door with a large key and they found themselves in a hallway with stairs going up to the first floor. On their left was another entrance door which opened a moment later. A woman stood on the threshold of the ground-floor flat, welcoming the three people and one dog and inviting them in from the hallway. Leon moved in, as happy and excited as he was anytime he discovered something new. Etta, Dora and Nathalie followed.

Freja and Magnus Holm were both tall with straight blond bro flow hair. Etta thought that if it weren't for their clothes, she'd hardly be able to distinguish one from the other. Freja, who had to be in her mid-fifties, was more than happy to show her guests the whole flat – that is, after inviting them to remove their shoes in the long corridor and put on felt slippers from a wicker basket hanging on the wall at the entrance.

The comfy living room had ancient wooden floors and was warmed by a stove. There were plenty of bookshelves, and Christmas decorations and candles lit up the darkened windows. The room had no central light, but a number of reading lamps were strategically placed in the corners to create a cosy atmosphere. Plenty of pillows on the sofa and armchairs and a large Christmas tree that was visible from outside completed the feeling of festive homeliness.

The kitchen was splendid in white and blue faience tiles. Its door gave access to a patio and a small garden at the back of the house.

"From the cobbled street outside, I'd never have thought there could be a garden here," said Dora.

"Ærø is full of surprises, you'll see," said Freja, happy that her two Italian guests seemed to be enthusiastic about her home.

From the kitchen counter, Magnus uncovered a tray of delightfully colourful open sandwiches.

"I prepared a few *smørrebrød* for our aperitivo," he said.

"They look gorgeous," cried Dora, her mind already taking notes of all the ingredients so she could replicate them once they were back home – to the shock of most of their neighbours, who were convinced that you could only eat real food in Italy. "What are they made with?"

"The base is always rye bread – you'll discover that we're keen on it in Denmark."

"Indeed, I enjoy its coarse texture and will miss it when I'm back in Castelmezzano, where it's not that common."

"Yes, you have your durum wheat there, but here it's rye almost all the time. As for the rest of the sandwich, whatever takes your fancy: butter, yogurt and herbs or some other spread. These are made with local smoked salmon," Magnus moved his finger from one row of sandwiches to the next, "herrings, cheese and eggs. Then you can add salad: radish, red onion, cucumber, bean sprouts..."

"There's lettuce, prawns, dill and beets on mine," said Etta, tasting a mouthful.

"Pickled onions with cheese on mine, but there's something sweet, too."

"A spoonful of cane sugar when I caramelised the onions." Magnus winked at Dora.

"Woof, woof, WOOF!" protested Leon. Weren't they forgetting someone? Just because he was polite and educated enough not to jump over the kitchen counter and help himself to the feast, wasn't he allowed to know what Ærø's dishes tasted like, too? Humans could be so tactless at times.

"You're right, young fellow," Magnus apologised, putting a couple of *smørrebrød* in a bowl that Dora had produced as if by magic. It did not matter how many there were, the *smørrebrød* seemed to disappear as quickly as the bowl had appeared.

"Let's sit at the table in the living room, dinner is ready," said Freja.

Whilst they were eating the fish soup, the Holms were happy to share with their guests what life was like on the island.

"In our spare time," Freja said, "we're both members of an association that welcomes people to the island. If anyone thinks of coming to live on Ærø, we provide them with accommodation for a short time so they can get to know what life here is really like before making a final decision."

"We contact homeowners," continued Magnus, "asking for furnished and comfortable accommodation. There's a lot involved as people might come from anywhere and have very different needs according to their culture and customs."

"Why are you so eager for more people to move in?" Etta asked, thinking she would be happy to share the island with as few people as possible.

"It's like this, you see," Magnus answered. "The more residents there are, the more tax money the island gets and the better the services will become."

"And mostly," added Freja, in perfect synchronicity with her husband, "the island can stay alive all through the year."

"We're very grateful to tourists, who now come during the off season, too."

"But to keep hospitals and schools open, we also need new residents."

"Yes," said Dora sympathetically, "it's the same in Castelmezzano. We're so far from big cities that young people tend to leave, not necessarily because they want to, but because they can only find a job elsewhere and long commutes are tough, especially when you have a family."

"That's why we're extending our invitation not only to skilled workers who can help with the islanders' needs, but also artists and remote workers in search of a cheap and peaceful place to live. In other words, people who won't miss the mainland as they can work from anywhere."

"And maybe bring their families along too."

"Or we can find them prospective husbands or wives," laughed Magnus.

"I'd love to marry on the island and live here for the rest of my life," said Nathalie with dreamy eyes.

"You're not a native?" asked Dora.

"Oh no, I live and study in Copenhagen, but am here to complete my six months' internship with the local tourist board. Once I've done my degree, I'd love to carry on working here. My colleagues at the office have been so welcoming, and life on the island is so peaceful."

"I wondered," said Etta, "if the place might be *too* peaceful for a young woman."

"Not at all. When I was a child, my father worked on oil rigs, so my life has involved moving every couple of years to a new place." She laughed. "Maybe because of that, I crave stability."

"I thought," said Dora, "you and Flemming's children were old friends. They seem very attached to you."

"Emma and Thomas have grown fond of Nathalie," confirmed Freja with a teasing twinkle in her eyes.

"I augment my earnings," Nathalie said, flushing slightly, "with some side hustle jobs. I started as a waitress over the weekends, but I definitely prefer taking care of young children rather than the drunken older ones at the end of the week."

"And what do you do in your spare time – that is, if you have any left?" asked Etta, for some inexplicable reason feeling an affinity with this smiling young woman.

"Clubs and associations are a must on the island. I joined the bikers' club, and throughout the summer, we visited most of the islands in the archipelago. I'm learning to knit, although I'm not that good at it, and every Thursday, I swim with the winter bathing club."

"Winter bathing?" Etta asked in surprise. "Are there any thermal waters around Ærø?"

"Not really." Nathalie laughed again, her dimples deepening, her fringe jumping around. "We swim in the open sea."

"In winter?" For Etta, it was hard to believe that people could bathe in the Baltic sea during the summer, although she had almost been persuaded to test the waters in Mecklenburg in June.

"I was swimming this very morning. And people of all ages come along. It keeps you fit, your skin smooth, and you're sure not to catch a cold for the whole winter."

"That is, if you survive pneumonia."

"You can come with me next Thursday."

Etta shook her head, horrified, while Dora, maybe in an effort to keep warm, concentrated on her fish soup. It was delicious, with a strange, yet exquisite taste. She couldn't decipher what it was and felt compelled to ask her hosts.

Magnus gave another of his deep, gentle, velvety laughs. "Well spotted. The fish fillets are marinated in lemon, saffron… and aquavit, our local spirit."

"It tastes good," Dora acknowledged.

"Yes, that's fish the Viking way."

More dishes and dessert left them sleepy and satisfied, and even Etta wondered if it was really true that Italian cuisine was the best in the world. Who said so? Maybe her neighbours who had never travelled further than Naples. She conveniently forgot that, until she had started travelling with Dora a few months earlier, she had been one of their number.

Dora, trying not to doze off, went to have a look at the bookcase. Most of the books were in Danish, but still she enjoyed recognising authors' names and identifying the novels. It felt so intimate, looking at what another person chose to read. She found a section of older books and couldn't resist opening a few to see the year in which they had been printed, and to admire the colourful drawings.

"Are you a lover of books?" Freja asked her.

"Yes! Well, mostly I love folk tales from around the globe."

"Then you should have a look in the attic. I used to rent it to the local antiquarian. She emptied it recently as she's moved into a larger house along the coast and has got her own storeroom there now, but she left a few boxes of books. She says people hardly buy books any longer and was going to throw them away, so I told her I'd try to find a home for them. You can sort through them and see if there's anything to your liking."

An attic full of old books was an invitation from heaven for Dora.

"I'll have a look tomorrow. I'm collecting *Pippi Longstocking* editions from every country we visit so it'd be lovely to find a copy in your house."

"I don't think I've seen any of those, but there are definitely some Scandinavian folk tales. Beautifully illustrated, too."

"You might want to keep them for your grandchildren?"

"I'm afraid it's more we oldies who go in for such things these days, so feel free to take any you like. I've already selected a few for myself, so you won't be denying me any treasures." Freja looked at her watch. "My goodness, time flies between a chat and a morsel of food. But before we leave, there's a few things I want to show you about the house."

The 'training' session for a house swap starts with the mundane things such as how to use the washing machine and dryer, how the rubbish collection system works. Then it goes through the idiosyncrasies, such as setting the bread toaster to one, because two will turn your bread to carbon. And that's after Magnus had repaired it.

"Oh, and if you hear a big clang during the night," Freja continued, "don't worry about it, it's just the boiler. It happens once a week or so and apparently it can't be fixed."

But once the household trivia is over, homeswappers finally get to the interesting stuff: a folder each host creates sharing their insider tips, such as the best restaurants, cafés and bakeries in the area; the lesser-known walks; the local attractions that shouldn't be missed; the favourite places of all kinds. This folder was a secret benchmark from which to enjoy the most breathtaking vista, the most exhilarating ramble, the most curious of shops, the best bargains at the market.

With their heads still spinning from the amount of

information they'd just received, Etta, Dora and Leon accompanied their hosts and Nathalie to the door and said goodbye to Freja and Magnus, wishing them a safe journey and a pleasant stay in Castelmezzano. Then they stood in the living room, happy and satisfied with their new accommodation.

"What should we do now?" Dora asked.

"Woof, woof, WOOF!" insisted Leon.

The two women looked at each other. After a whole day of travel, the Basset Hound deserved a walk in the neighbourhood, not to mention the fact that they too were curious to see what Ærøskøbing had to offer, even if it meant enduring the frosty air of a Baltic winter's evening.

4

A SPOOKY ATTIC

After a long walk, Dora, Etta and Leon were happy to find their house warm and inviting. They drank a cup of hot tea while Dora eulogised about what she had just seen: the cobbled streets reflecting the light of the yellow lamps; the green garlands going from one side of every street to the other, sparkling with little lights; Torvet – the town's main square – surrounded by charming buildings, including the Town Hall and local library, their brick façades splendid with elegant arched doors and windows. The long Vestergade street, the shorter but equally enchanting Brogade street connecting the main square directly to the harbour. Passing by cute houses where the windows had no curtains, they'd peeped into the cosy interiors, always glowing in a dim, warm light.

Fearing Dora might spend the rest of the evening lost in a world of imagination about what she'd just seen, Etta tried to bring her back to reality.

"Shall we go up to the attic and search through those books?"

"At this time?"

"It's not that late, and I don't want to switch on the TV and spoil such a perfect evening."

"Why not?" said Dora, thinking that she might find her Danish copy of *Pippi Longstocking* despite what Freja had said. "Let's go."

Leon sprang up, thinking an even longer walk was on offer. He was always ready to go; it didn't matter where, the simple act of going somewhere new was his *raison d'être*.

"It's just upstairs," Dora warned him.

Leon was partly disappointed, but not too much. After all, he'd never been up in the attic. As they passed by the door to Nathalie's flat, he stopped to smell it, just to make sure he knew exactly who lived there.

Etta opened the door to the attic, which was as powdered with dust and cobwebs as attics tended to be, and switched on the light. There were a couple of small openings – you could barely call them windows – set in the roof, but it was too dark outside from them to cast a light onto anything.

"It's cold," said Dora as a shiver ran down her spine, despite the fact that she and her friend were both wearing fleeces as they had expected a chill in the air.

Unlike other attics, though, this one was almost empty. Just a couple of pieces of furniture – a bookcase hiding the back wall completely, an old ebony writing desk with an oil lamp on top and a half-open toolbox on the floor next to it. And there, in the middle of the room, stood three large boxes.

"Those must be the books..."

"Let's have a look," said Etta.

"Now?" asked Dora.

"Well, that's why we came."

"I know, it's just..."

"Just what?"

"It's a little cold, and the place is not as... cosy as I had imagined." The truth was, Dora was feeling rather uncomfortable, but it was hard to explain why. Just as the rest of the house – the downstairs flat they were staying in, the halls and the staircases – felt welcoming, the attic seemed hostile. Shaking her head, she cast the thought away. It was just that she was tired and cold, neither one ever a good companion.

Etta, indifferent to her friend's tribulations, was already extracting the books from one of the boxes and putting them on the empty bookshelves so that Dora could check them one by one.

"*Little Women, Anne of Green Gables,* a series of Jane Austens… all translated into Danish," Dora murmured, fascinated, touching the old yellow pages, smelling their musty scent.

"Jules Verne's *Around the World in Eighty Days,*" cried Etta.

"I'd love to do such a tour nowadays following in Phileas Fogg's footsteps," Dora replied.

"*Twenty Thousand Leagues Under the Sea, Treasure Island,* and wait, isn't that *Dr Jekyll and Mr Hyde*?" Etta said, handling a book with a torn cover. Browsing through the first few pages, she knew it was exactly that.

"It's mostly children's literature," commented Dora, a bit more enthusiastic now, though still a little ill at ease.

"Let's move on to the second box," Etta said, clapping her hands to get rid of most of the dust that had accumulated on them. "You will love this one! Here are the tales of the Brother Grimm with beautiful illustrations. And these must be Scandinavian legends."

Dora was now feeling excited. She had a passion for folk tales; her only regret was that she didn't speak any Scandinavian languages so she wouldn't be able to read them directly. Then she sent up a shriek that made both Etta and Leon jump.

"What now?" Etta asked.

"*East O' the Sun and West O' the Moon,* in such a beautifully illustrated book!"

"Is it in Danish?"

"Maybe Norwegian, but look at the illustrations of the castle and the young lassie. As for the bad Long Noses, they look really scary. I'm sure children would appreciate that."

"I know the tale," grumbled Etta. "Not one of my favourites at all."

"Why?" asked Dora in wonder. There was so much scope for imagination in the story – what could be better for young children?

"Well, the strong young lassie goes through all sorts of adventures. She meets old hags and furious winds, manages to arrive east of the sun and west of the moon, settles in with the terrifying Long Noses..."

Dora looked at her impatiently, waiting for the grand finale.

"And then all the prince does," concluded Etta, "after having slept like a log for years, is say he will marry the one who can wash his shirt clean from three spots of tallow!"

"What's wrong with that?"

"Don't you see? You can be as strong and brave as you like, but all men want in a woman is a meek housewife!"

"Woof, Woof, WOOF!" Leon jumped up all of a sudden and pointed to the attic door.

"What does that hush puppy want now?" Etta wondered. "We're not going out again until tomorrow."

"Maybe he just wants to head back downstairs," said Dora. "And I'd be happy to comply. The cold is getting a bit too much for me."

"We haven't gone through the third box..."

"We can finish tomorrow. Was there any tea left?"

"Yes, I covered the pot with a tea cosy. Hopefully it's still warm, otherwise there's always the microwave."

Dora shivered, but not from the cold this time. She had never thought that any good could come from warming up your tea – or anything else, for that matter – in a microwave. When the attic door closed behind them, she felt a sudden relief, and Leon was clearly happy to return to their cosy accommodation and go to sleep on his pillow in Etta's bedroom. He had made up his mind he didn't like that attic at all.

5

ÆRØ BEACH HUTS

"You can't ever leave!" cried a terrible woman with a pendulous nose at least 50 centimetres long, a ring around it. As she spoke, she slammed the attic door shut, leaving Dora alone, trembling in the dark and hostile room. Moments later, through the thick blackness, something cold, wet and menacing grabbed her around the neck and the terrified woman screamed with all her might.

And it was her own scream that woke her up in the middle of her large four-poster double bed. Leon was leaning against the side, his front paws up, looking at her in dismay. Usually it was the grumpy biped who shouted and made a fuss; this other one tended to be rather softly spoken.

"Oh Leon, it was you and your wet nose," Dora laughed. "But this time, you gave me the fright of my life!" And as she said this, she took the large head of the dog in her hands, looked into his irresistible droopy eyes and smacked a kiss onto his forehead.

Leon wagged his tail as he tried to break free. He didn't like indulging in mawkishness for too long, just in case someone thought he was not really the tough guy he portrayed. And more importantly, it was morning and there were so many things to get done. They were in a new place with plenty of neighbours to get acquainted with, nearby parks to be discovered, long rows of trees to be marked so that other dogs knew he was there. And of course, he had to see if there were any lovely she-dogs around. The life of a Basset Hound is not for the faint of heart.

"What's going on?" Etta asked, poking her head into the room.

"I'm sorry if I scared you, Leon gave me a fright while I was still sleeping. What time is it?"

"Half past eight."

"It looks like it's just after dawn."

"It is. Dawn in Ærø is at 8.15."

"I had forgotten that. Shall we accompany this chap outside?"

"And have a cappuccino and a pastry at the bakery Freja suggested?"

The two women nodded in unison.

ONCE OUTSIDE, THE DOOR CLOSING AT HER BACK, Etta had the strange feeling they were being observed. She looked around; no one was in view, but out of the corner of her eye, she thought she caught a small movement of the curtains in the other half of the building that they were staying in, the ground-floor flat next door to theirs. But she had no time to confirm her impressions. Leon was pulling his two bipeds towards the Vestergade, where he followed the street down to the harbour. It was a set rule that the two women would allow him to choose the route for the morning walk. And Leon did remarkably well, as if he'd always lived on the island.

There were still quite a few boats in the marina, but Leon did not pay them any attention. He was concentrating on the grass aplenty he found on a walk amongst the beach huts. A few fishermen were busy cleaning and hanging their nets on wooden racks. They smiled at the three newcomers and greeted them.

"People are more friendly here than in Copenhagen," Etta acknowledged, her voice tactlessly loud. One of the fishermen overheard her.

"Ay, Missus, here on the island we're folks of the world. They say we're the Southerners of Scandinavia because of our openness and desire to talk to strangers. Maybe it's because the sea connects us with the whole world."

The man asked where they were from and said he had visited Italy a few times. He knew the harbours as a sailor, the cities as a tourist.

"With my wife, I visited Sorrento and Amalfi – such pretty, sunny places. I wonder, what has brought you to the harsh North?"

Dora pointed to the marina and put her hands up to her ears to listen to the breeze, the metallic clanging sound as the wind gusted between folded sails and masts. She shielded her eyes and looked up at the soft northern light. The sun was still low and pale, but it raised little swirls of steam on the sea, tickling the wings of a few ducks sleeping on the water. The light of dawn separating the sky from the sea was a marvel!

The man nodded in approval. "I guess we have our share of magic here, too."

"Are these the celebrated sea cabins?" asked Etta. She was rather disappointed at the red and grey huts not too far from them.

"Nay, Missus, these are the modern ones. You have to walk further up to Vestre Strandvej for the older ones," and he set them on a path amongst luscious green meadows. They were lucky as Leon had a mind to go in that direction, too. Etta set him free and his whole body shivered in excitement. Plenty of enticing smells, the cold dew on the blades of grass, huge spaces to trot and gallop across – Ærø was a dog's heaven.

Against the line of the horizon, they saw a long string of colourful cabins spaced a small distance apart from each other, rather like summerhouses facing the sea. Each was little more than a kitchen table packed inside four walls and a roof, but they were striking nonetheless. One was a brilliant violet, another was lemon yellow; one had red and white stripes, the next had the smallest but most charming porch with white framed windows and door against dark red walls. One was a denim blue with items from the sea displayed on the windowsill, another was a bright green with delicate curtains. And in front of these cabins was a sandy white beach that could compete with a tropical island's.

Dora stood frozen, clasping her hands. Etta panicked, hoping her friend wouldn't get over-emotional and start crying. Luckily, Dora just breathed deeply through her mouth, gasping as if she was a cod suddenly pulled from the ocean, and drank it all in.

Leon took advantage of his bipeds' lack of attention to launch himself into a run across the beach. He galloped as only Bassets can, his ears flapping up and down as if they were long wings readying themselves to take flight. But instead of flying, he stopped abruptly as he stumbled into a heap of clothes.

Dora and Etta watched the scene unfold. The heap of clothes didn't react under the impact, but the dog stood there in surprise, looking at Etta and Dora, inviting them to come closer and make sense of it.

"Goodness, not again," Etta murmured as her stomach tightened and all thoughts of breakfast abandoned her. "It's a curse." Dora didn't utter a single word as they both approached the dog.

A winter coat, a sailor's hat, some very old shoes.

"Homelessness is also a problem on Ærø, I see," said Etta,

but she hesitated to touch the figure inside the clothes. "Maybe he's just drunk?"

"Let's hope so. Why don't you give him a little shake?"

"Thanks a lot, Miss Pepe!"

With narrowed eyes, Etta stretched out a reluctant hand to where the figure's arm should be. The clothes were damp and cold. Beneath them, whatever it was, the figure was certainly not alive. Just still and rigid. Well, not so very rigid. At a stronger shake, to Etta's alarm, the body inside the clothes seemed to crumble between her fingers.

6

BLACK FRIDAY

Horrified, Etta shouted out loud. Seized by hysteria, Dora burst into frantic laughter.

For the first time in her life, Etta feared she might faint. Luckily, just before her mind faded out into thick blackness, she caught what her friend was saying.

"It's a sandman," said Dora, chuckling normally now.

"A sandman?" Etta's cry was even louder than her shout, but she recovered almost immediately.

"It must have been made by children with some old rags."

"I knew we should never trust this dog," and with that, Etta sprang to her feet, cast a nasty look at Leon and headed back towards the town centre. "I deserve a full breakfast now."

BACK IN THE HARBOUR, THEY MET UP WITH NATHALIE, who was just leaving the Tourist Information office where she worked. She asked them if they were settling in comfortably before inviting them to join her for a coffee.

"I can show you the best place to go for breakfast, then," she said.

"Is it OK for you to leave work?"

"Today is Black Friday. I need to take a few pictures to post on the Ærø Island social media, and I'll be interviewing businesses and tourists as research for my dissertation."

She took them back along the Vestergade, this time heading inland.

"I already love this street," said Dora, pointing to the colourful row of one storey buildings. "But what's that?" In front of a beautifully carved door with designs in blue and white stood a wooden fruit crate lined with a chequered towel in the same colours, two large tins containing transparent bags of homemade biscuits, sealed with red and green ribbons, inside it. Beside it, another crate brimmed with felt slippers in various shades of blue. Each item had a price tag, and between the two boxes stood a glass jar containing a handful of Danish krone.

"But there isn't anyone around," cried Etta, marvelling at the vendor's trust.

"That's the honour system on Ærø," Nathalie explained, as proud as if she were responsible for it. "You help yourself to what you want and leave the money in the jar."

"But anyone could steal the items or help themselves to the money."

"We tend to trust people on the island."

"You won't get much out of life if you trust folks."

"On the contrary," Nathalie replied. "Just knowing that you can trust people makes you happy."

"But if they don't deserve it, you're going to get hurt."

"One exception to the rule doesn't mean you cannot trust people. And there is quite a lot of research in scientific journals stating that those who trust the people around them end up having a happier life than those who are always mistrustful."

Etta was going to protest at this rather naïve assertion when it struck her that Dora was a case in point. The woman believed the world was populated by nice, trustworthy people and she had somehow managed to get through life, just like Etta herself had done. Only... only Dora seemed to have had much more fun in the process. Had Dora naturally embraced the *hygge* attitude to life? Was she more Danish than Italian?

Thoughts of people being happier than she was or capable of living life more easily never failed to make Etta feel rather uncomfortable. As she was trying to settle herself, keeping any bad mood hidden firmly inside, her companions were taking a seat in a quaint bakery café. People were queuing to buy their bread and who knows what other delicacies from a counter filled with all sorts of brioches and biscuits, the scent of cinnamon, vanilla and cardamom blending with the coffee aroma in an irresistible combination. The café had all the lights switched off, except the tiny Christmas lights on the decorations and the candles on the tables and main counter.

"Did you say Black Friday?" asked Dora.

"Isn't that more of an American tradition?" asked Etta. From the number of Danish flags she had seen in Copenhagen and along the Ærøskøbing streets, she had assumed the Danes were fiercely patriotic and therefore less inclined to welcome foreign traditions.

"We 'inherited' the parts of it we like and turned it into a special Ærø thing. As you see here, all the shops will keep their lights off all day."

Etta frowned so deeply that her red-framed glasses jumped off her nose.

"What?"

"Well, what I mean is they will keep the main lights off, so all shopping has to be done by candle or lantern light. Also, there is the first Christmas market this weekend..."

"It all sounds so exciting," Dora said, enchanted. It would

take her a long time to recover from so much cosiness around her.

"I wonder what you will dream about tonight," said Etta, as usual attempting to bring Dora back to planet Earth. "I hope you won't scream and yell again, the shock could kill me."

"What happened?" Nathalie asked, barely hiding a smile. Dora told her about her nightmare, how her brain had put the Long Noses from the fairy tale together with the uncomfortable feeling she'd had in the attic.

"I'm sure it was just due to the cold and tiredness. After all, we found a treasure trove of books up there."

"That place *is* creepy," Nathalie confirmed. "The children told me they used to go up there and they too found it frightening."

"Frightening why?" asked Etta.

"Maybe they thought they saw a ghost of some sort, or maybe Thomas made up some other story with the naughty purpose of scaring his sister."

"But how come Thomas and Emma visited the Holms' attic?"

"Their grandmother used to rent it from Freja, so maybe they visited with her."

"Their grandmother? From the way Flemming spoke, I thought he had no relatives left on the island."

"Well, Flemming's father was a sailor, mainly in Marstal, but he lived here until he died in a tragic accident a couple of years ago. Flemming's mother and father divorced a few years after they got married and she took their children back to live in Odense where she came from originally. But his mother-in-law lives here in Ærøskøbing."

"That's a good thing, he has someone to help out with the kids."

"I don't think so. He's no longer on speaking terms with her... which is a pity."

"Oh, that sounds awful!" Dora could not imagine staying, or even being mad with anybody in the family, maybe because she had so few relatives left. "How come? He seems such a gentle man."

"Probably because he's had no luck with his own family. His mother passed away in Odense when he was about my age, whilst his father always had problems with alcohol and apparently wasn't the best father, nor grandfather in the world."

"One's own children are often the toughest judges," grunted Etta.

"Guilty as charged," Nathalie said, looking at her with interest. "I might have been too tough on my own parents, too, but we have rather divergent opinions, especially my father and I. Mind you, I speak to them every day and we try to meet as often as possible, although within 24 hours, we'll probably be quarrelling about the most stupid of things..."

Etta thought of her relationship with her only child, Maddalena. It was not an easy one, either. She didn't mention it, but her eyes locked with Nathalie's and they smiled at each other guiltily in mutual understanding.

"So Flemming and his mother-in-law, they are not on the best of terms..."

"Unfortunately, they hardly ever speak to each other. They already had a difficult relationship when his wife was alive. I think it's because her mother did not approve of the marriage..."

"But that must have been years ago," said Dora. "Thomas must be around nine years old."

"Yes, but after Flemming's wife passed away, his mother-in-law tried to get custody of the children, and with that, their relationship collapsed once and for all. At least, that's what I managed to get out of him... It's hard to reconstruct what happened when someone is determined not to speak of it..."

"I thought he would confide in you."

"In this respect, Flemming is a true Viking," Nathalie said, resting her hands on her high cheekbones. The eyes peeping from beneath the fringe were twinkling with a tinge of irony. "They fear no battles, nor the toughest of sea storms, but ask them to talk about their emotions, their intimate thoughts, and they're as scared as little mice."

Dora laughed. "That reminds me of someone." As she pointed at Etta, Leon raised his head. "No, not this time. For once, I wasn't talking about you," she apologised. The Basset lowered his head again, wondering what bipeds had to talk about other than a brave and handsome dog. Really!

A young waitress, a huge smile on her face, her blonde hair tied in a messy knot on top of her head, approached them with a bowl and asked if she could serve a special *smørrebrød* with hardened rye bread and herring pieces to Leon as a snack. The answer being positive, the dog decided that life was worth living after all.

Silence fell when the fragrant *kanelsnegle* and *wienerbrød* – cinnamon rolls and Viennese breads, still warm from the oven – were served. But the aromatic hot coffee had the most special taste of all after the early morning cold.

~

AFTER NATHALIE HAD LEFT THEM WITH A LONG LIST of her favourite places to visit, the two women and one Basset Hound spent the rest of the morning discovering the town centre. They walked back to Torvet Square and admired the Town Hall and library. They took it in turns to explore the white Ærøskøbing church with its red roof. It was fat and squat, barely visible from afar as people on the island had never favoured tall bell towers that could signal the presence of a town to pirates coming from the sea.

Etta, to her surprise, enjoyed exploring the local shops,

maybe because they weren't as boring as shopping malls, nor as soulless as chain stores. As Nathalie had anticipated, that day they were all lit only by old lamps, lanterns and plenty of candles.

Dora insisted on visiting both the Flaske-Peters Samling Museum, featuring a collection of over 500 model ships in bottles, and Hammerich's House. The latter was the home of the great Danish sculptor Gunnar Hammerich, she explained to tempt Etta in. Hammerich had been the first to acknowledge the charm of Ærøskøbing and the importance of its heritage, and had set the basis for the preservation of the old buildings, never spoiling the town with new developments. Instead, he'd had the foresight to make the locals aware of the treasure they had all around them.

The house contained a plethora of antiques as the man used to travel a great deal, hunting for treasures, but it was in front of his collection of 3,000 Dutch tiles that Etta – standing in the cold with Leon on the leash, peeping through the window – feared her friend had turned to stone and would linger there for the rest of eternity, so powerfully did Dora clasp her hands and so immobile did she stand. Luckily, Dora slowly turned to flesh and bone again so they could make their way home with their few bags of food and a first round of Christmas shopping. On the way, Emma and Thomas, riding their bikes, called to the two women, their father following close behind them.

On Friday, Flemming told them, he finished work earlier than usual, and so did the children at school, as the Danish system believed family life was just as important, if not more important than working life. Etta protested that if people put shorter hours in at work, the country's productivity would suffer. Flemming shook his head firmly and told her that even larger Danish companies didn't expect employees to work long hours. Instead of a performance review, they'd be sent out to

Time Management classes if they found it difficult to finish their job during their work hours.

"Maddalena, my daughter, would love this attitude," said Etta. Her rebel daughter had never complied with the common 'wisdom' of spending one's whole life at work, sacrificing family time.

"And how are you getting on in your house?" asked Flemming, recognising an argument he was never going to win and looking at the red-brick building behind them.

"Oh, it's lovely," said Dora. "I can't wait to get our stove going and sit and read a book next to it."

"About books," Etta had been waiting for this moment, "we found plenty in the attic last night." And she looked up at the tiny windows in the roof. "But what a *spooky* place!"

Flemming translated the word spooky for the children, but there was no need. Thomas had picked up on it eagerly.

"Oh, it's very spooky. We used to call it the moving room."

"Moving?" asked Etta.

"It moves around. Actually, it is the walls that move backwards and forwards, making it look larger, then smaller."

"I see," replied Etta dubiously. She noticed Flemming frowning.

"Maybe you're getting confused with the flat next door where Granddad lived," he said.

"No," Thomas said, shaking his head, "Granddad lived at 47 on the first floor. This is Freja's home, number 49, and I meant Grandma's attic there."

"When were you in that attic?" Flemming asked, his voice serious.

Thomas flushed slightly. "We went up there with Freja. Remember the time when you used to leave us with her because we had no childminder?"

"I didn't know you'd gone into the attic, though."

"Only a couple of times when she had to check things for Grandma."

A dark cloud seemed to pass over Flemming's face, then he shrugged and his customary smile appeared again.

"And remember, we're expecting you to come for dinner at ours tomorrow," he said to Etta and Dora. "We're going to cook some delicious food," he added, shaking two large bags in the front basket of his bike.

"That sounds lovely," said Dora. "And I will take care of the dessert, I will make something special for these two," she smiled at the children

"And Nathalie is coming too," Emma announced.

"Now, let's leave these lovely ladies and their handsome hound to go and warm up a bit," said Flemming. Indeed, even Leon thought the time had come for a nap. He'd done plenty of work for one day. But not Etta. No, Etta had... well, let's just say other things on her mind.

7

BACK IN THE COLD

"Don't take your coat off," said Etta as soon as they'd put all their shopping bags and packs down in the kitchen. "Let's see if we can finish looking through the books in the attic."

"No way!" an unusually determined Dora answered. "I'm not going back in there now. It's cold, and even worse, it's dark."

"We've gone through most of the books already, I'm sure it won't take long."

"Etta, please, can we do it tomorrow morning? And what's this interest in the books all of a sudden?"

Finally, Etta confessed. "I feel like there's something I should have noticed and didn't. I want to have a look."

But when Dora shook her head stubbornly, Etta knew this was one of the very rare occasions when the people pleaser said no, and there was no chance she would change her mind.

"Then I'll go with Leon," she said.

Leon, who had settled himself comfortably on his bed – a pillow temporarily placed on the living room floor – opened his right eye with a smirk, as if saying, "I'm not coming, either, so why not give up on your crackpot idea and get that stove on?"

There was central heating in the house, but – and in this, Leon thought like Dora – the warmth of a stove was altogether cosier.

"Come on, Leon," Etta repeated, her confidence dwindling. This time, the dog didn't even bother to open one eye, instead pretending to be fast asleep.

"I know you're awake," Etta said, irritated. She opened the front door in the hope that some primeval instinct would cause Leon to spring up, as he had done every time the outdoors was on offer in the six months they'd lived together. But nope, this time it seemed all neural connections were broken and Leon continued snoring as if nothing would ever wake him again. Meanwhile, Dora had removed her winter coat and was busy preparing some hot tea.

"Traitors!" Etta growled, slamming the door behind her and walking upstairs, her steps not as decisive as she would have wished. She was tempted to make an excuse to stop at Nathalie's flat on the first floor and ask her to come along, but she forced herself to abandon the idea. She couldn't take another no!

The last flight of stairs was dingy, musty and uninviting. She opened the door, and in her solitude, the attic looked emptier and colder and grimier than the day before. About to retrace her steps, she thought of the two turncoats downstairs enquiring whether she'd accomplished her important mission. She'd better find something worthwhile, something that would make them forever regret that they hadn't come along and had missed all the fun as a result.

Fun?

"What the heck was I thinking?" Etta told herself, glancing around the desolate room, unable to retrace the thread of her earlier thinking. Why had it seemed so important to come up here immediately? She was cold, lonely and scared, while she could have been sipping tea, munching Christmas biscuits and chattering next to a roaring stove.

The dim light of the bulb hanging from the wires in the ceiling showed the three boxes of books, the toolbox, the old writing desk, the bookcase with the few books they had left the previous night.

"OK, keep your cool, you old hag. You've had a hunch, I know you've had a hunch, you just don't know why," she kept her voice much lower than usual. She needed to speak to encourage herself, but not too loud in case she woke something evil from the silence around.

She went over to the old desk, searching every compartment and drawer, then pulled them out and checked their backs. A secret hiding place – wasn't there one in all the best mystery novels? If there was, it had to be *very* secret because she couldn't find it. She moved on to the bookcase, searching for a lever to reveal a hidden passage, touching all the shelves, picking up dust and cobwebs on her fingers. But she found nothing, except...

"Oh my!" she said in disgust, seeing a dead spider, all crumpled up and sticking to her palm.

The third box of books. That was all she had left, the only place that might possibly be hiding something to show the two renegades downstairs how wrong they had been not to follow her. She just wished the box wasn't so large.

Twenty-plus minutes later, Etta was colder, lonelier and angrier than ever, and what was worse, she had found nothing. Meanwhile, the two traitors were enjoying the comforts of Freja and Magnus's flat. She imagined Dora in her armchair, reading a book, a hot cup of tea between her hands, the stove burning. But not for a second did the thought strike Etta to stop her vain search and go back down to join her friend. In her determination to find something of significance, she was unaware that nothing was keeping her in the dingy attic but her stupid pride.

Creeping noises made her jump. Surely, it was nothing but wood lice, but the sinister sounds made a worthy companion to the unpleasant feeling of being observed, and of ever increasing dread.

"Enough!" she finally burst out, heading resolutely for the door as the light went off. She stood frozen, holding her breath and waiting for something terrible to happen.

Nothing.

Etta timorously reached out for the wall with her fingertips in search of the door handle to freedom. Her heart thumped dreadfully in her chest, almost choking her. It took ages to find the door. Finally, her mind in a frenzy of fear, Etta's trembling hands differentiated the wooden door from the cold brick and timber of the wall. Seconds later, she was grasping the handle, pushing it down… but the door did not open. Fired by adrenaline, a reactive grey cell in her brain supplied the useless information that she'd stupidly left her mobile phone downstairs. Then she was left with pure, thick black panic.

She screamed with all her might, stamping her feet, hoping Nathalie or her flatmate or whoever was at home would hear her. She doubted Dora or Leon would. And the more desperate she became, the louder her cries got as she alternately banged against the door and stamped on the floor, screaming all the time.

Moments later, a voice sounded from the other side of the door. "What's the matter?"

"I can't open the door, the lights are off," Etta cried, never having been happier to be close to another human being.

"You must have locked it from within!" the voice answered firmly. It was Nathalie.

"I haven't."

"Please, keep your cool and search for the key. Are you sure it's not in the lock?"

"Of cour…" her fingers ran below the handle and she found a key, and a second grey cell reminded her that she, Concetta

Natale Passolina and no one else, had locked the door, fearing someone might sneak up the stairs and take her by surprise.

She turned the key, feeling more stupid than she ever had in her entire life. Nathalie was startled when the door opened all of a sudden.

"But how come you were in the dark? No wonder you couldn't find the key!"

"The light just went off as I was about to leave."

"Oh my goodness, thinking you were locked in this dreary room can't have been the most pleasant of experiences. But you could have switched on the other set of lights," Nathalie said, searching then pressing a second switch. One bulb had gone, but another one was now shedding light from the opposite wall. The attic looked just as dingy as before, but less scary to Etta now that another human being was beside her.

"Sod off – that's to me and my stupid stubbornness," she explained hastily to Nathalie, turning her back on the attic and vowing never to re-enter the place ever again. But as she turned to close the door for the last time, her eyes fell on the bookcase. The very bookcase she had explored inch by inch, finding nothing. Only now… it looked different.

"What's that they say about the trees and the forest and you can only see one or the other?" she asked Nathalie.

"You mean, you can't see the wood for the trees?" Nathalie suggested.

"Yes, something along those lines."

"And what's the wood or the trees in this case?"

Etta did not reply. The window – the window was so close to the wall that housed the bookcase. A third grey cell flashed an image in her brain of Thomas looking up at the little windows of the attic when they were in the street earlier on. From there, it had seemed there was a certain distance between the window and the wall separating one building from the other.

Etta instantly recovered from her panic and fear. "Look at

that window, so very close to the bookcase." She gave Nathalie just enough time to take notice. "Now, let's go downstairs. We need to check it out."

Nathalie wanted to say, "Check out what?" but she decided not to, just in case the red-haired woman had lost her mind. Better to humour her.

"Let's leave the light on," said Etta. "Otherwise we won't see much on this darkest of Black Fridays." And with that, she sprinted down the stairs with surprising agility for a comfortably plump retired teacher, the young woman trotting obediently behind her.

Once they were out in the street, Etta let out a victorious cry.

"That's it!"

"What?" Nathalie asked, not noticing anything particularly worthy of her attention.

"Upstairs, the bookcase at the end of the room is next to the window. But from here, it's clear there's a good metre and a half between the window and the partitioning wall separating the Holms' property from the next."

"That's true!" Nathalie acknowledged.

"There must be something behind the bookcase. Let's go back upstairs and see if we can move it forward, find out what's there."

"Why?" asked Nathalie. "Maybe Freja and Magnus have their reasons to..."

"I wonder if they know. Thomas said he and Emma got scared because the room had moving walls that made it large, then smaller. Adults thought it was just his imagination, but the child was right. The room was smaller because someone had moved the wall and the bookcase forward, and from what I understand, at that time it was Flemming's mother-in-law who rented the attic."

Nathalie acknowledged that fact, but failed to see the importance of such a minor discovery. Nonetheless, she followed Etta upstairs. In short zigzagging movements, they pulled now the left side of the bookcase, now the right, managing to move the piece of furniture forward. Etta squeezed herself behind it, but there was only a wall. It was not painted, but was still a wall.

"I'm sorry," said Nathalie, "but it looks like we were wrong."

Without bothering to answer, Etta knocked on the wall. Her knock echoed into empty space.

"A bit too thin to be a main wall, don't you think?"

"The house next door and this one were originally part of the same building. Maybe when it was divided, they decided they didn't need a thick wall."

"It doesn't make sense. On the ground floor, there's a thick partitioning wall. Downstairs, we can hardly hear a sound from the neighbours. And if we imagine the wall going all the way up to the roof, it shouldn't be here at all, but at least a metre further down."

As they spoke, they became aware of a faint smell that seemed to rise from the wall. It wasn't strong, barely perceptible, but it was sickening.

"So what?" Nathalie asked, her patience at an end.

"What if we see what's behind it?"

"How?"

"We make a little hole in the wall."

"What if we make a little hole into the next building?"

"We will apologise and say we were trying to hang a painting or carve out a niche or whatever."

"Shall I open the windows?" Nathalie said, doing just that without waiting for a reply. "This room is already cold, so a bit more won't matter, but this strange smell – I can't bear it any longer. That's better!" she said, breathing in the chilly fresh air from the small window.

"Let's see if there's something in the toolkit," Etta said. Moments later, she came back holding a small sledgehammer. A few bangs made a little hole in the drywall sheets, and from within came a slightly hissing rush of air, as if gas was escaping. The smell wasn't much stronger, but still nauseating.

"I hope we won't find a family of rats putrefying in there," said Nathalie with a disgusted grimace on her face, wondering why she had bothered to come and help this curious lady at all.

"Do you have your mobile?" Etta asked when the hole was about 30 cm in diameter. "I need a torch."

"Of course not, I ran up as quickly as I could when I heard you screaming, but I'll go and fetch it."

"I will wait for you on the stairs; I don't want to be alone in here even for a second. And maybe you could get a couple of pairs of gardening gloves in case we need to tear part of the wall down."

Nathalie, quick as a flash, left Etta at the top of the stairs, and within minutes they were standing side by side, shining torchlight into what looked like an empty store room. As Etta had said, the partitioning wall was a little more than a metre away. There were no windows in this portion of the roof. But mostly, the space was disappointingly, desolately empty.

"Maybe it was just a way of insulating the two attics," said Nathalie.

"Insulating them from what?"

"I don't know, but it's a small space with no doors or windows. I can't see any other purpose for it."

"Wait! What's that? Shine the light in the far corner."

"There?" said Nathalie, pointing the light towards the furthest corner whilst Etta tried to squeeze her face into the hole next to the young woman's phone.

"It's a bundle of rags, I believe, almost the same colour as the floor."

"Let me see," and it was Nathalie's turn to look inside. "Not sure, is that a coat lying on the ground?"

"I think we need to get in!"

Nathalie stood beside her companion, a little unsure. Did they have a right to proceed? After all, neither woman was the owner of the house. But she couldn't deny she was starting to feel curious about the whole business, too.

"Do you think it might be important?" she asked to quieten her lingering doubts.

"I can't say until we know what's in there. So, do you have anything bigger than this sledgehammer at your place?"

"I don't think so, shall we check downstairs?"

"Nope, I'd rather not alarm the other two. It's only a dry wall, we can proceed with this. It will just take a bit longer."

It actually only took a few minutes before a full section of drywall between two wooden studs had been torn down. With trepidation, Etta bowed under the horizontal cross stud and squeezed between the vertical ones, wishing she were thinner. She entered the small space, Nathalie's mobile phone torch in her hand, and kneeled down beside the bundle of tatters.

Nathalie was right, it was nothing but a ragged coat. Etta wasn't going to be fooled again as she had been on the beach. From the hem of the coat, what looked to be a shoe emerged. In a sudden flash of inspiration, Etta moved the torchlight from the shoe all the way along a string of buttons on the coat until she reached the collar, where she was met by a dazzling 32-tooth grin.

For the second time that day, she let out a powerful scream.

Nathalie started in panic. "What is it?"

Etta barely had the heart to reply.

"It's a skeleton!"

8

A PROMISE IS MADE TO BE BROKEN

"I'm not sure I've understood. Why did you pull the bookcase forward, see a wall and decide to tear it down?" a sturdy policewoman with a flat, expressionless face asked for maybe the fourth time. Her smaller colleague was a tad more sympathetic, but he clearly had no power whatsoever to control her.

Etta was sitting on the couch in the ground-floor flat, Dora having covered her knees with a blanket and prepared a cup of hot tea with more sugar than liquid in it. But it had done her some good.

"I told you, I noticed the window was not in line with the inner wall. If you go out of the building, you will see what I mean," Etta said once more with uncharacteristic patience, showing she was still in shock and not her usual self.

"People don't generally go around breaking down walls in other people's houses, whether they are aligned or not. You must have known you'd find something. Tell me what you knew, and how."

"I've told you again and again, but it seems to me you're determined not to listen!"

"You're hiding things from the police, that's not a good idea."

"I only arrived on the island yesterday and I've found the remains of someone who must have been missing for quite some time. What more do you want from me?"

"So you knew about the skeleton before you arrived on Ærø, did you? Maybe that's why you came here."

"Yes, I'm a tourist of the macabre. I only visit places where I know I'll find a cadaver hidden somewhere. I made long searches online at home, then spotted the skeleton on Google Maps and decided the island..."

"I knew it! Finally, you confess."

The policewoman's colleague spoke to her in Danish, maybe suggesting Etta was joking. But she was determined to enjoy her triumph.

Etta decided she'd better avoid sarcasm. The woman was, after all, a police officer with the power to send her to prison if something convinced her of Etta's alleged guilt. Irony and hunch were obviously two words not included in her vocabulary.

It was then that another officer came in. He greeted Etta with a smile and a nod, and then asked the policewoman in Danish what she had found out. A shadow passed over his face as she reported her findings, using the word Etta recognised as meaning *information* time and time again. Then he looked at the junior officer, who apparently offered a different explanation, using the word *nysgerrig* to describe Etta. It was not too dissimilar to the German *neugierig* – inquisitive. Etta's German was still quite good, so she tried to make out as many words as she could. Was the policewoman saying that she was withholding information whilst her shy colleague was supporting Etta, saying she had an inquisitive mind? Inquisitive – such a good word. She actually felt pleased with that description, but which of the two versions would the senior officer trust?

The officer nodded and winked at her, then sent the policewoman to run some errands and sat in front of Etta with a smile, the junior officer still at his side. Maybe it was good news after all.

"Mrs Passolina, I'm Lucas Knudsen, the officer in charge of the investigation."

Etta nodded. She couldn't help notice that he was rather handsome: tall, athletic, dark blond with a winning smile. She could hardly imagine a starker contrast with the obnoxious, short, dark-haired, pig-headed Maresciallo Gaggio back home in Castelmezzano.

"I wanted to thank you for your important contribution today."

"I thought by way of thanks your colleague was going to arrest me," and Etta nodded towards the door through which the policewoman had left.

"I'm very sorry, Vera is old school. She's a good cop, just lacking a little… imagination."

"Not to mention humour."

"True! On the other hand, you seem to have plenty of both…"

"Just as much as one needs to get through life with one's sanity intact."

"Maybe a touch more than that. Or at least, that's what it seems, as no one else has ever thought of searching for a body in that attic."

"*I* wasn't searching for a body," said Etta, now wondering if behind all his politeness, he wasn't trying to frame her.

"Then would you explain to me what you were searching for and why you looked behind that wall?"

Etta sighed heavily, mostly because she was starting to see that her actions did sometimes take her into places that were a little beyond common logic. Feeling less pugnacious than usual, she made one more effort to explain. She told Knudsen that their host Freja Holm had invited them to look at a few books in the attic, how the room had given them the creeps from the outset, how Leon had wanted to leave, how young Thomas Grøn had mentioned the attic had moving walls and that had attracted her attention to the position of the windows on the roof, both from the inside and the outside. And finally, she explained how the mismatch had led her to think there could be a secret chamber between the two buildings.

"That's excellent work," Knudsen said. "I wish you had been here a couple of years back."

"Why? What happened then?"

"I might as well tell you as I'm sure most islanders will let you know just as soon as I leave. Two years back, a Polish woman came to the island. She was an amateur archaeologist – you know, the type of person who goes onto historical sites with metal detectors, hunting for ancient coins, jewels or weapons."

Etta nodded. Yes, she'd seen such people hunting for treasures from times past, but not disparaging modern coins or jewels if that's all they could find.

"She was keen on Viking history and booked to stay on the island for a week. She had no close relatives, but her friends raised the alarm when she didn't return home."

"You think the body might be hers?"

"That's the only missing person case we've had in recent years. The skeleton you found looks rather small and this corresponds to the description we have of the woman. We need the pathologist to do their analysis, see if they can find any more details on her body for a definitive identification. But personally, I feel there's a good chance it's her."

"Oh my goodness!" was all Etta could say. She was silent for a while, but her brain was an unstoppable machine. Once the surprise had passed, she came to the only possible conclusion. "But if she was hidden in the attic, that means it must have been foul play."

"Whoever the skeleton belonged to, it can only be foul play."

"Did you suspect something bad had happened to the archaeologist at the time?"

"We weren't sure, but we found no evidence pointing in that direction. No one had seen her after she'd left, but she had cleared her rented house in Ærøskøbing, so she could have disappeared on the ferry, maybe thrown overboard by someone else or herself, or maybe she had just chosen to disappear once she was back on the mainland. All hypotheses remained open, but one thing was sure: she never made the flight from Copenhagen back home to Gdansk."

"Did she know anyone on the island?"

"Apparently not, though during her stay, she spoke with a few locals."

"Did you suspect any of them?"

"Not really, but let's make one thing clear," said Knudsen, shaking his head. "We don't know what happened, neither then, nor now, but we can't ignore the fact there's possibly a killer still here on the island. You've done all you could as a good citizen, but now you have to step back and let the police continue their investigations."

"Of course," said Etta, lying without compunction.

"If the person who committed this crime is still around, he or she is dangerous. I want you to promise me – solemnly swear – that you will drop any snooping you may be tempted to do right now. Enjoy the island like any other tourist."

"Of course," Etta said again, raising her right hand in the universal sign of a promise and crossing her left hand's fingers under the blanket.

Lucas Knudsen smiled, satisfied. "I'd better leave you to recover from the shock, but I need you to come to the police station tomorrow, here in Ærøskøbing. You will find your statement ready to be signed, and you might want to add things if you remember anything overnight."

"I will," said Etta. "How about Nathalie?"

"We've questioned her, too, and your two versions coincide, which is a good thing. Even Vera will come to the same conclusion."

Etta looked at him seriously. "Will I meet her at the station tomorrow?"

"Ask for me," and with that, Knudsen gave her his card, and then he and the junior officer left.

9

CONSPIRACY THEORIES

As soon as the police left, Dora came in to the room to comfort Etta. Leon, on the other hand, looked at her with a certain reproach in his eyes.

"Didn't I tell you not to go into that attic?" he seemed to say. "I smelled that it was no good, but nope, you had to stick your nose in, and see what it got you?"

"Are you feeling any better?" asked Dora.

"I think so. Actually, if you get your laptop, we can search for articles on the Polish archaeologist who disappeared from the island..."

"Who?"

Etta was updating her friend on what the Chief Inspector had told her when someone knocked at the door. It was Nathalie, wanting to make sure Etta was OK.

"I am," she said from her armchair.

"And how are you?" Dora asked Nathalie, offering her a cup of hot, sweet tea.

"Still feeling I'm in a book rather than real life. I've been living for almost six months in the same building as a hidden cadaver – incredible on such a peaceful island!" But it was hard to tell if it was horror or curiosity lightening the sparkles in her eyes.

"I think we should update Freja and Magnus," said Etta.

"Do you want me to phone them?" asked Dora, fearing her friend was still too much in shock to hold a conversation over the phone.

"I think one of us should, but before that, Nathalie can help us to go through a few local articles. I imagine most will be in Danish. We're investigating the disappearance of a Polish archaeologist," Etta told Nathalie, pointing to Dora's laptop. Nathalie said she might have heard about the woman's disappearance, most likely on the national news while she was living in Copenhagen. But she didn't remember that the woman had gone missing from the Island of Ærø, possibly because the place didn't mean anything to her in those days.

Dora handed the young woman her laptop and Nathalie quickly found a few articles with the name of the victim. In October just over two years earlier, Agnieszka Kamiński had vanished from the island. She had been seen chatting to locals at the Ærøskøbing Pub the evening before her disappearance. The bike she had used to explore the island had been found where it belonged at the house she had rented, but all her stuff had gone. The landlady of the accommodation just thought the woman had left to return home, exactly as she was due to that day. If Agnieszka's friends had not raised the alarm in Poland, no one on the island would have taken any notice that the woman had gone.

From evidence supplied by ticket control on the Ærøskøbing–Svendborg ferry, it seemed Agnieszka had taken the morning ferry. But had she continued by coach or train to Copenhagen? She hadn't bought a ticket with her credit card, so all the police had done at the time was to ask the public if anyone had met her on the ferry or train. No reliable witness had come forward.

The three women looked at each other.

"But if she took the ferry, maybe it's not her body after all," said Dora.

"Someone might have used her ticket to create the impression she'd left the island," Etta observed.

"They don't check your ID onboard," said Nathalie. "They just scan your ticket."

"Then there would be nothing easier," said Etta, "than for someone else to sell Agnieszka's ticket at the harbour, saying they couldn't travel for some reason and therefore had a spare ticket..."

"And if a visitor bought it, no one would be any the wiser," completed Nathalie

"But what was Agnieszka's body doing in the Holms' attic?" Dora asked.

It was time to give their hosts a call. As her manners were the softest, Dora decided she would do all the talking.

Freja thanked her and said that Chief Inspector Knudsen, to whom she referred by his first name, had already phoned her. When questioned, she had remembered that the week the Polish woman had disappeared, she and Magnus had been away visiting their daughter in Copenhagen. It was on the news that they had learned about the woman's disappearance on Ærø; it was rare that the island would come up in the national news for anything other than a festival or other tourist event. Lucas Knudsen had then asked if she'd been renting the attic at the time, and also who'd occupied the first-floor flat, where Nathalie now lived.

Etta made a sign to Dora that they too wanted those names. Freja said that Sille Skytte was renting her attic, whilst the first floor had been occupied by a female artist.

"Ask her name and if she's still living on the island," hissed Etta.

"Camilla Egede," Dora repeated the name as Nathalie took

notes. "She left Ærøskøbing and Freja isn't sure if she's still on the island at all."

When Dora ended the call, Etta was already making plans for the next day, but first she wanted to make sure she had got things right.

"I take it Sille Skytte is Flemming's mother-in-law?"

"Yes, that's her name," said Nathalie thoughtfully. Now that murder had struck this close to people she cared about, she wasn't sure she was as enthusiastic about their snooping as she'd been before.

Etta too was thoughtful. The name of Flemming's mother-in-law had jogged a memory that was refusing to surface. Then Etta's busy mind raced on and the memory faded back into the mists of time again.

"So if they found a body in the attic she was renting at the time, we might assume – and certainly the police would assume – she had something to do with the murder."

"That'd be awful!" Nathalie cried.

"Well, you told us she's no longer in touch with the children. Maybe their father sensed all along that she wasn't a good influence on them…"

"Maybe she isn't the nicest character ever, but she's still their grandmother…" Nathalie looked at the two older woman uncertainly. Dora had one of her hunches.

"She's still seeing the children, but their father doesn't know."

"What?" asked Etta.

Nathalie squirmed on her chair. "Well, all that started before I got to know them. She was meeting the children when she knew their father wasn't in the vicinity."

"Did Freja Holm have a role in this?"

"Yes. At times, she'd offer to look after the children at her place, and then she'd let Sille know they were free to meet. When I started to look after them, they told me their big secret.

I didn't see anything wrong with it; actually, I thought it would be a good thing for them to see their grandmother, as they'd already lost their mother..."

"So you helped in this clandestine scheme, too?" Etta asked her.

"I'm afraid I did. At times, we'd meet Sille outdoors, pretending we'd just happened to bump into her on a walk. Or I'd leave the children to play in the garden, and she'd stop by and chat with them. I knew their father wouldn't approve, but it was just for a few minutes. At times, she'd bring them a doughnut each, or a book or small toy, and I'd pretend to Flemming that it was something he must have bought them a while ago and forgotten about."

"You said Sille Skytte tried to get custody of the children. I take it the court didn't grant it."

"Actually, the court never got that far because Sille withdrew her request. It was Freja who intervened and told her how wrong she was being, but by the time she relinquished her claim, Flemming was determined his children should have nothing more to do with her. I know Freja has spoken to him time and time again, but the man is pig-headed."

"If Sille Skytte killed a woman, Flemming might damn well be right."

Dora frowned at Etta for using such strong language, but her friend hardly took any notice.

"Of course, we never suspected anything of the sort. The worst thing is the children are going to be awfully hurt should it turn out she's involved in such a heinous crime. But why would she be?"

"The Holms mentioned an antiques shop," said Dora, remembering the conversation at dinner when Freja had invited them to have a look at the attic.

"Yes, Sille owns an antiques shop in the town centre. It's a pretty good one, too." Nathalie looked at the two women whose gazes had become even more serious and concerned.

"So Sille's got an antiques shop, and we have someone going missing while they were treasure hunting on the island. The two things might be connected. It's a good starting point. What if Agnieszka found something important and went to speak to Sille?"

"So what?" Nathalie shrugged somewhat petulantly.

"Agnieszka Kamiński," Etta snorted impatiently at having to explain the obvious, "showed Sille Skytte something precious – so precious that the woman decided to do away with the Polish archaeologist so she could get her hands on it."

"But I've seen what these metal detectors come up with: a few coins if they're lucky, maybe a brooch or other fragments. No one would kill a person for that."

"Obviously, Agnieszka found something better than that."

"In which case, she would have alerted the authorities."

"Oh no, much better to alert an antiques expert. The authorities would have taken her discovery and given her nothing in return; with Sille, she could have struck a deal. I'm sure there's a market for some things these amateur archaeologists find."

"But that'd be illegal…"

"And so is murder."

10

THE ANTIQUES SHOP

The next morning, Leon made sure to lead his humans to discover another part of Ærøskøbing. He pulled them down the Vestergade towards the harbour; Etta and Dora imagined they were heading towards the cabins on the Vestre Strandvej again, but Leon turned to the right.

Etta stopped. She wanted to speak to the fishermen she'd seen on the marina the day before, but as she pulled on the leash, Leon moved backwards, bent his neck and, with a strange manoeuvre only he could have perfected, slipped his collar.

He moved ahead, but didn't run away, his body pointing towards where he wanted to go, his head turning back to the women as if to say, "You stubborn pair, don't you want to come along?"

Etta contemplated the empty leash she was still holding and the collar on the ground. She picked it up and put the collar back on Leon's neck, deciding it wasn't worth going against his wishes. She had learned the dog could turn into a heavyweight mule if she tried to get his bum to move a millimetre in a direction he didn't want to go.

"After all, we did say we'd allow him to lead the party for the morning walks," she said. "But now it seems the hound wants to decide when to be on the leash, too. I wonder why Sauer didn't call him Houdini." Sebastian Sauer, the late Night Watchman of Rothenburg, had been Leon's previous owner before being brutally killed. The dog, though heartbroken, had taken the opportunity to adopt Etta and Dora as his new servants.

Leon had managed to find a coastal path winding between the pretty frontages of early 20th century villas on the right and stunning views of the sea and the coastline on the left. As Dora clasped her hands, alternately breathing in the morning air, touching the moss on the tree trunks and falling into a trance as she listened to the seagulls' cries in the sky, Etta made sure they'd get something useful out of the walk. Using Leon as bait, she spoke to every single dog owner who came their way.

If Dora hadn't been lost in dreams, she'd have been amazed – she'd never have seen Etta so amiable and sociable. Everyone who stopped to speak to this friendly lady knew about the grisly discovery, and one even hinted that the body being found in that particular attic was a tell-tale sign as to who the guilty party was.

"With that temper of hers, it comes as no surprise at all. She broke her daughter's heart, then committed this terrible crime."

"What do you mean, she broke her daughter's heart?"

"Sille Skytte didn't want her daughter to marry Flemming Grøn; she had greater ambitions for her, wanting her to go to Copenhagen and work in some high-profile job, rather than marrying a primary school teacher. Not to mention how she opposed their decision to move to the island. Her poor daughter died of leukaemia shortly afterwards, and what did the woman do? Try to gain custody of the children!"

"Oh my goodness!" cried Etta.

"She's got a heart of stone."

"But we heard she dropped her claim..."

"Maybe her lawyer told her she'd have no chance of being successful. But she caused poor Flemming a great deal of worry when he already had enough problems of his own, bringing up two children all by himself while grieving for his wife. Now the time has come for justice to take its course."

The woman walked them to a beautiful yellow villa on their right, a white fence bordering a long strip of perfectly kept garden. The villa had a large porch with two white arches, green-framed doors and windows. On the upper floor, a little terrace running underneath the roof connected a door and two windows, each of which had a stucco surround surmounted by a white arch. Two marble busts decorated the balcony's railings. Under the pointed roof, a white label indicated 1910 as the villa's year of construction. The usual Danish flag was flapping in the wind beside the house.

Dora kept her cry of admiration at how pretty the villa was to herself. She could imagine the joy of waking up there in the morning, savouring the view over the sea from the terrace with a cup of hot coffee in her hands.

The woman, less poetic than Dora, whispered, "That's her house. Sille Skytte's. She bought it years ago, but she had the expensive renovation work done in the past couple of years, soon after the Polish woman disappeared. And that says it all..." She let a meaningful pause linger in the air, giving the two Italian women time to come to their own conclusions.

At that moment, a tall, robust woman pushing a heavy wheelbarrow appeared from one side of the garden. She stopped near a low brick wall and carried out some repair work.

"Is that Sille?" asked Etta.

"No, that's Tina Thorning, Sille Skytte's assistant in the shop. She's been helping her with the house, too, moving in and doing all the necessary repairs. Sille's totally enslaved poor Tina, but I've said more than enough." The woman cast a look at her little dog and said, "We'd better move on, Veronique."

To the huge disappointment of Leon, Veronique followed her owner and the two disappeared from sight.

"I remember Freja telling us Sille Skytte has a storehouse at her new home, which must be in the back garden. That's why she decided to clear the attic," said Etta, looking at the robust Tina who was now disappearing towards the back of the house. "At the same time, leaving the attic free ran the risk of someone finding the skeleton. Not that it was an obvious hiding place, but still, while it was her space, her secret – if indeed she was the culprit – couldn't have been safer... no one would go nosing around."

The path continued on and on. Cultivated fields had taken the place of the houses, but a powerful grumble from three empty stomachs told the explorers it was time to go back home. Despite being hungry, Leon was opposed to the idea of returning until the word 'breakfast' was explicitly mentioned. Of course, you can give up something as good as an inspiring walk if you know something better awaits.

~

ON THE WAY BACK, THEY LOOKED AT THE VILLA, BUT there was no sign of life.

"Maybe they've gone to the shop," Dora suggested.

"We'll find out soon enough, we need to pay Sille Skytte a visit."

Etta had asked Nathalie the shop's address, not that it would have been difficult to find it in Ærøskøbing, so small was the town. But the more organised you are in life, the less time you waste.

Etta hesitated on Vestergade at the turn onto their street. "Perhaps we could just have a little look to make sure the shop is open and see what Sille looks like." They passed a side street already bustling with activity, sellers setting up their Christmas market stalls, the alluring smell of cinnamon pastries coming from the nearest bakery. In one of Ærøskøbing's oldest buildings, they peeped in the windows of the antiques shop, recognising Tina Thorning, the shop assistant. She was alone.

"I'd say it's time for a late breakfast," said Etta resolutely. They sighed a little as they resisted the temptation to go into one of the quaint cafés, but they had to reconcile their long trips with the thin pensions they received, and eating most of their meals at home definitely helped. Though a coffee and cake stop later in the day was something they could indulge in.

They were out again as soon as they had eaten to make the most of the daylight hours. It had been their intention to visit the Ærø museum, which was enchanting, but the whole experience of walking anywhere in Ærøskøbing was like walking in a lively open-air museum. The town was full of little corners and quaint views to admire; inevitably, Dora stopped before long to take in the sight of pretty pastel walls, wooden doors in bright colours and a multitude of different decorations. Some charming buildings, such as the *Philip Kock Hus*, the oldest house in Ærøskøbing, dated from the 1600s. Its long, skewed roof boasted a tiny window, and bright orange walls contrasted with the dark wooden beams of its half-timbered structure.

By the time they returned to the antiques shop, it was almost lunchtime, but the lights were already on. Etta peered in through the window – luckily, she hadn't walked straight in as she recognised the woman on the other side of the counter. No wonder the name Sille had stirred a memory from its resting place – it was the same woman she'd had a squabble with on the ferry as they arrived on Ærø.

"How silly of me!" Etta said. "I should have realised it was her. The stewardess who rescued me called her by her name."

"And she was the woman Flemming hurried the children past. He was, in fact, making sure they ignored their grandmother," Dora said. "It's such a sad story, two grown-ups who could help each other and, more importantly, make the children happy insist on fighting with one another."

"I guess it happens more often than you might think. It seems to be in human nature to make someone's life miserable rather than better. Still, we need to speak to her."

"Do you think so?" said Dora, not too keen on talking to someone who had most likely killed a woman for the sake of some golden coins or ancient jewellery.

"Well, I say 'we', but I can't exactly walk in. I'm sure she'd recognise me and I'm afraid we've already had one heated quarrel. But you're so sweet and gentle, Dora, I'm sure you'd get on like a house on fire."

"But I can't ask her what she was doing two years ago when the treasure hunter disappeared…"

"Of course you can't, but you can walk in, ask for a few prices, appreciate some of that dusty old stuff, and then say something about how peaceful the island is… and see how she reacts."

"But she won't fall into the trap. She won't say a word about the skeleton being found if she had a role in the murder."

"Then her reaction will be interesting as she will be the first person we've met today who hasn't mentioned the skeleton we found yesterday. That must mean something, surely?"

Dora looked at her friend with great respect. The way Etta's contorted mind worked won her admiration.

"Shall I leave Leon with you?"

"Yes, I'm sure she's not the kind to appreciate dogs or any pets."

Smiling inwardly – Etta had been the least appreciative of pets of anyone she had ever met until Leon came into their lives – Dora passed the leash to her friend. As she took hold of it, with her free hand, Etta pointed to a mirror between the shop door and the window.

"What's that?"

"That's one of Ærø's mirrors. Make sure the shop owner doesn't see you waiting for me with Leon."

"You're right. Still, it seems to be so perverted, using mirrors to spy on people."

Dora laughed. "There are plenty of them in Ærøskøbing, Nathalie told me about them. Apparently, the reserved Danish people would rather not go out when their neighbours are in the street, thereby avoiding idle chitchat."

Etta felt like banging her forehead with her hand; the Danes were strange creatures indeed. But was the idea really all that alien? This kind of reserve might be exasperating for any other human being, but for Etta, the mirrors suddenly made perfect sense.

~

DORA, OUT OF VIEW OF THE TELL-TALE MIRROR, DID her best to smooth her hair and adjust her clothing to assume a convincing air before finally entering the shop. The tingling of a bell announced her arrival.

"Good morning," Tina Thorning said. Imposing by virtue of being tall and robust, she had a surprisingly mousy voice compounded by a dull face. "Can I help you?"

Dora was startled as her eyes had been concentrating on the other woman sitting at the counter, the one Etta had recognised. For her part, Mrs Sille Skytte barely acknowledged Dora's presence, a curt nod of the head her only greeting. Perhaps, Dora decided, it would be better, or at least easier, to strike up a conversation with the woman's assistant first.

"Yes please, I'm looking for a few presents to take home to my family and I'm in need of ideas." She looked around. The shop seemed to be full of precious things: portraits in gilded frames of austere people from times gone by, elegant alabaster lamps, not to mention the refined pieces of furniture, so Dora felt obliged to add, "Not very expensive ones."

The shop assistant stopped in her tracks and something close to an indulgent smile appeared on her face. She changed direction, moving from the most precious items to a little table in the corner of the shop laid out with trinkets: porcelain coffee cups, silver spoons, insignificant costume jewellery, a row of mundane Dresden figurines and candle holders similar to those Dora would find in any bric-à-brac market back home. But above the table was a wall-mounted cabinet containing old books. Dora felt a little hope rising in her.

"I wonder if you happen to have a copy of *Pippi Longstocking*?"

"We might have, but I'm afraid it won't be in English. Most likely German..."

"I'd love one in Danish, if possible."

"Do you speak Danish?"

"Not at all, but I collect a *Pippi Longstocking* book from each country I visit. I so hope to find a Danish edition."

"That's an unusual collection, what a lovely idea. Let me check out our books."

As she said this, Tina marched over to the counter, exchanged a few words in Danish with the owner, then came back with a stool. She climbed onto it and explored the dusty bookshelf one book at a time.

"I'm afraid we don't stock Pippi Longstocking. Maybe you should try the local bookstore. They will certainly have a modern edition, but I believe they also have a selection of second-hand books if you're searching for an older one."

"I certainly will," said Dora, wondering how she could keep the conversation going. As kind as the other woman was, Dora felt the presence of the owner was somehow making both of them feel uneasy. "Would you mind if I were to look around? I'm so fond of nice things, and I've noticed a couple of desk lamps that are really pretty."

"Of course, you're welcome to browse, and if you need any help, just give me a call," and Tina retired unobtrusively to a little table where she had all she needed to make antique silver shine.

Despite the Christmas tunes playing on the sound system, there was a sombre atmosphere inside the shop. Maybe it was just that a lack of customers meant there was no buzz of conversation, no people commenting over this item or that. Muffled laughter came from the stalls outside, but the antiques shop, as such shops tend to be, was rather too much on the quiet side.

The door bell rang once more as a couple walked in. Before the shop assistant could offer her service, the woman halted her and said in German they just wanted to have a look. The owner, Sille Skytte, frowned as if she didn't like people coming in to browse, a silly attitude for any shop owner, thought Dora. Sille had stopped checking her records and was keeping her eyes on the new visitors and Dora.

Not a word was exchanged between the owner and the shop assistant, but when the bell rang for a third time, Sille's sigh of exasperation was clear evidence that she didn't appreciate visitors.

The new arrival was Nathalie. That was too much of a coincidence for Dora to believe that Etta hadn't sent her to help.

Nathalie went to say hello to Sille. They exchanged a few words, but despite the young woman's smile, Sille seemed to be rather distant. Then Nathalie turned towards Dora as if surprised to find her there. She introduced her to Sille, telling the shopkeeper that Dora was one of the Holms' guests. Dora walked over and shook hands with Sille, then Nathalie introduced Tina.

"She's been working with Sille since..."

"It's almost ten years," the woman said in her monotone voice.

"Tina and I attend the same winter bathing club. Will you be swimming next Thursday?"

Tina, her grey hair flat against her temple, hinted at a smile as she nodded a yes.

Then Nathalie got straight to the point. "Coincidentally, it was Dora who found the skeleton in the Holms' attic. Everyone's talking about it. I wonder how it got there."

There was a long moment of silence. Tina looked at her boss as if fearing a strong reaction on her side. Then the bell broke the silence as the two German tourists left without making a purchase, or even saying goodbye.

"Good day to you, too," said Sille sarcastically as the door closed behind them. "It's only polite to acknowledge people when you come into and leave their shop."

Undeterred, Nathalie pressed her point. "Sille, I believe you used to rent Freja Holm's attic, didn't you?"

"Yes, I used it as a store room."

"Then I wonder, could anyone else gain access to the attic? Did you ever find things went missing when..."

"Nathalie," Sille interrupted her icily, "I've already been questioned by the police, and as you can see, I'm back here so they clearly didn't see any reason to arrest me."

Nathalie flushed beyond crimson. "I didn't mean that, of course. But can you imagine what a shock it was to us to move the bookshelf and find poor Agnieszka Kamiński, the Polish woman who went missing two years ago? The police haven't said anything about how she was killed, have they?"

"They didn't mention it to me. And how do you know it's the Polish woman? I didn't think the police had formally identified the body yet."

"I can't see who else it could be. It's not like lots of people go missing on Ærø. So, did you ever speak to her while she was here?"

"I did," Sille replied reluctantly. "She came over to show me some of her findings. They weren't that interesting, at least not for my shop, and I told her so."

"What were they?"

"The usual – buttons, a few coins, fragments of a brooch…"

"And did you advise her to try somewhere else?"

Sille considered the question, maybe taking time to construct a careful answer.

"I reminded her that in Denmark, whatever you find that is older than 100 years is public property and has to be handed in to a local museum, letting the curators know where it was found."

"So you advised her to get in touch with the Ærø Museum?"

"Exactly."

"But maybe that's not what she wanted to do, which was why she came to you rather than going to the museum…"

"Possibly. But I don't sell archaeological findings in my shop, unless they're part of a private collection and I have proof of that through documentation. Otherwise, it is against the law."

"Maybe as she was Polish, Agnieszka didn't know that?"

A sarcastic smile appeared on the older woman's face. "Of course, she did. If you are a metal detectorist, you need to know the rules in every country you visit." She paused, snorted rebelliously as if to say that she'd had enough of this second interrogation, and then volunteered a final snippet. "Whether you respect the rules or not is up to you. But you have to know them beforehand." Then she turned to Tina. "Where are you with that silver? Mrs Henningsen is coming to collect the cutlery set today, it's a present for her daughter-in-law."

"I'm almost finished," Tina answered, turning her attention back to the silverware she had been polishing. And with that, Nathalie and Dora knew their interview time was over.

11

PLANNING AN INVESTIGATION

As soon as Nathalie and Dora joined Etta and Leon, who were waiting for them a little way up the street, they all decided to go to a café to share their findings. Etta rapidly calculated that a bowl of soup would not cost them a fortune; there are times you simply can't scrimp and save, and a café wouldn't charge as much as a fancy restaurant.

Leon insisted on going back to his favourite bakery, but was dismayed when it was a waiter and not the cute blonde waitress who served them. He threw himself down on the floor in disappointment, and when the man didn't even bring him any *smørrebrød* with herrings, dejection became despair.

"So the two did meet," said Etta, indifferent to the dog's tribulations as she listened to Dora and Nathalie recount what they had discovered in Sille's shop. "And Agnieszka did find something during her searches. It might be two years on, but the culprit should be crystal clear, even for the police."

"Oh, don't say that," Nathalie protested. "I know Sille can come across as a harridan, but she's not as bad as all that..."

"Well, I met her on the ferry over to Ærø," replied Etta,

wondering why there was always at least one person ready to defend an obvious criminal. "And I can tell you she's an aggressive troublemaker at the very least."

"I know she's blunt, but there's a big difference between that and murder."

Etta's eyes were piercing through Nathalie. "And why is that you're so clearly on her side?"

"She's Thomas and Emma's grandmother. Those children have already lost their mum, they don't deserve any more bad luck!"

"If she were a killer, it'd be better for them to know now."

Dora was going to contest this hotly, but Etta interrupted before she could voice her thoughts.

"I don't mean we should go and tell them brutally, 'Your grandmother is a killer'," she said impatiently, exasperated at having to justify her words. "But their father already wants to keep them apart, so they won't miss her as much as they would if she played a big part in their lives."

"It's still a bitter pill," Dora said.

"I wonder if Flemming's negativity towards Sille is because he knows or suspects something."

"Please," implored Nathalie, "that'd be even worse! Poor Flemming, he's had more than his fair share of worry, it would be so unfortunate..."

The waiter brought over three bowls of soup, served with a basket of warm, dark bread, fresh butter ready to spread and a little salad in a side dish. He asked if the dog would enjoy some toast, and when the women nodded in approval, Leon accepted his dish with a nostalgic expression, as if thinking of the better times in his life.

"Talking about the truth," said Etta, her eyes fixed on Nathalie's face, "I'm not sure you've been completely honest with us. Why are you so concerned for those two children?"

Natalie's cheeks were on fire, her fringe not long enough to hide the glowing redness.

"What do you mean?" she asked, more to buy time than anything.

"I've a feeling you know what I mean!"

The young woman sighed; Dora looked at her encouragingly.

"You know, it might do you some good to talk about it, even if only to two old hags."

"Oh no, you're not hags; you're like a couple of dear aunties! I really feel I could confide in you..." She buttered her toast slowly. "Well, not that there's too much to tell. I'm afraid I have fallen in love with Flemming, and I adore his children. I dream of him asking me to marry him and we can all live happily ever after on the island." She chuckled to soften the impact of her confession.

"And have you spoken to him about this?" asked Dora seriously.

"Of course I have, but he thinks I'm too young and it's just an infatuation." She paused, her knife still on the bread, to take a deep breath. "Which, of course, it's not!"

"Such a shame," said Dora, "and the children are so fond of you."

Nathalie smiled at her with gratitude. Etta, as always, was pragmatic.

"OK. But if Sille is guilty, both Flemming and the children will have to cope with the brutal truth. One cannot gloss over a murder."

"I know, but I'm sure the police will deal with that. They will investigate Sille Skytte thoroughly, so I'm sure we can leave that work to the professionals..."

"And what work should we keep for ourselves?" asked Etta sarcastically. In truth, though, she enjoyed the way Nathalie expressed herself.

"Maybe we could do some sleuthing on the side, perhaps investigate other hypotheses."

"Such as?"

"Let's assume that Sille is innocent. Who else might have had an interest in killing a treasure hunter who had just arrived on the island and had found nothing but a few useless buttons?"

"Tut-tut, Nathalie," Etta said. "If you base your sleuthing on the wrong assumptions, I'm afraid you won't get very far as a detective."

"You mean, the body might turn out not to be Agnieszka Kamiński?"

"No, I'd say that is a most likely hypothesis, but you said she had found a few useless buttons. In which case, I don't believe she would have gone to Sille at all. I have half an idea she found something more significant than that, but if Sille mentioned the law like she did with you and Dora, that certainly could have put Agnieszka off."

"So we believe she might have found something of value?"

Etta nodded. She was holding a cup of coffee; in typical Italian style, she would never have a cappuccino after a meal. The black liquid was good, although not as good as an Italian espresso, but she was coming to terms with the fact that coffee tended to resemble broth in some countries.

"Then she was looking for a buyer?"

"Yes. She knew it would be risky trying to sneak old jewels home in her luggage – what if they checked her at the airport? So she was looking for someone who would be interested in her discovery."

"And that someone wasn't necessarily Sille?"

"I believe she was her first stop, but after Sille turned her away – if that's true – Agnieszka went somewhere else. We can investigate this hypothesis because the police, as you mentioned, will be doing all the necessary checks on Sille."

"All of a sudden, you sound so professional," Nathalie said with admiring eyes.

"I'm starting to wonder," replied Etta, pushing her huge red-framed glasses back up her nose, "if we shouldn't turn our private investigating into a profession."

Dora nodded in agreement.

"You mean it's not the first time you've looked into a murder?" the young woman asked.

"Since we retired, strange cases just seem to have fallen into our laps." With a nonchalant gesture worthy of the classic black-and-white Hollywood movie stars, Etta waved all their past successes away. "But now, we need an action plan."

She took a napkin, shook the bread crumbs from it and drew a rather ugly picture of a house with three floors.

"The body is here in the attic, but we're assuming Sille, who had easy access to the place at the time, was not involved in the crime. The question is, therefore, who was? Who else had access to the building?"

The pencil moved down to the ground floor.

"Not the Holms. True, they're the homeowners, but they've got an alibi that the police could check anytime. Their mobile phones, credit cards – all those dreary technological things can prove that they were away from home when Agnieszka was on the island. But what about Camilla Egede?" Etta's pencil moved up to the first floor. "Freja said she was living in your current accommodation, Nathalie. Would she have had access to the attic keys?"

"Everyone in the house knows that Freja has spares of all the keys in her study and you can access that most of the time from the back garden..."

"You can access the study?" Etta asked.

"I don't think she ever locks it."

"Even when she goes away?"

"People on the island aren't worried about break-ins like they are elsewhere..."

"But if Sille stored antiques in the attic, she might not have liked her stuff to be so easily accessed."

"She certainly didn't store precious jewellery or other smaller items in there, and who would steal a large painting, an old lamp or a piece of furniture? Their crime would be exposed as soon as they hit the street."

"That's true," Dora said with feeling. Ærø seemed to be such a perfectly peaceful place... well, except for the owner of the skeleton, of course.

"OK, we need to find out more about Camilla Egede. Does she still live on the island? Can we speak to her? That sort of thing. Nathalie, maybe you can take care of that. We should also consider how easy it is for someone who already has access to the house to get into the garden, fetch the keys and go up to the attic. But we can't overlook the fact that anyone might have known where Freja keeps the spare keys. It wouldn't take much to climb over the garden fence and access the study. What if the Polish woman showed or talked about her findings to someone in a pub, for example?"

"It will be hard to track him or her down two years later..."

"Unless it's someone else in the business. Someone as likely as Sille to be consulted if treasure trove were found..."

"And that someone wanted to sell it illegally, now I see what you mean," Nathalie jumped up, clapping her hands, startling the people in the café who glanced at her. Leon sprang onto all fours. Anytime he heard an audience – even a one-person audience – clapping their hands, he thought it was applause meant for him, a legacy of his past life as a canine actor with the Night Watchman of Rothenburg. The young woman sat down again with a sheepish grin on her face.

"That might not have been the best of starts as we really need to keep a low profile," said Etta, but it wasn't the serious rebuke most others would have suffered from the blunt woman. She liked Nathalie. "We should speak to an expert."

"An expert in sneakily selling archaeological findings?" Nathalie asked.

"Well, yes. It would be great if you could come up with a name."

The young woman shrugged. She had no idea, but they could speak to the Ærø Museum director. Surely he could shed some light on how someone could profit from treasure trove, if they were so inclined.

Etta regretted not having been able to speak to Sille Skytte herself. Her two companions had been a little naïve in their questioning. Hadn't the antiquarian mentioned that museums ask for the location of archaeological findings? Most likely, Sille too had asked the treasure hunter where she had found her trove, at least the area. In fact, couldn't anyone have asked, then followed the woman and done her in? Could the killer have decided to hide her body in town to pass the suspicion on to someone else?

Making a snap decision, Etta asked Nathalie to go back to Sille and acquire the missing information. Nathalie objected shyly.

"She can turn really nasty…"

"If she ends up in police custody, there will be no way for any of us to speak to her. With this in mind, go and do what you have to do."

"Oh my goodness, Sille in a prison cell, how could you suggest that?" But Nathalie did not wait for an answer. She knew deep down it was a possibility.

~

ETTA AND DORA APPROACHED ÆRØSKØBING MUSEUM at Brogade 3. To their surprise, it was quite easy to get to speak to the director, who was a she rather than a he. A friendly, charismatic woman, she took them into her office and explained to them how the Danish system worked, confirming what Sille had said.

"In Denmark, whatever you find that is older than 100 years is considered *Danefæ* – literally, dead ownerless property. As such, it belongs to the National Museum. Detectorists have to report their find to the relevant local museum, together with an explicit description of the circumstances and place in which it was found."

"Will the museum pay the treasure hunter?"

"Of course," the director said, as if proud of the fairness of the system. "It's not market value as that tends to reflect private interest or transitory fashion, but it's a fair price."

"And the museum pays the searcher immediately?"

This time, the woman guffawed at Etta's impertinence. "With the popularity of metal detectors, at times, the treasure hunter might have to wait up to a couple of years, but that's an extreme case. What I want to stress is that they can be sure they will receive their money in the end. And they don't have to go all the way to Copenhagen; any local museum can receive the findings."

"Does this include your museum?"

"Exactly." With another glow of pride, she went on to illustrate the fairness of the Danish system, a real win-win situation. "The government has thrived by being as generous as possible. Some countries have banned metal detectors almost completely, whilst Denmark adopted a more pragmatic approach. You see, most discoveries in non-archaeological areas come from detectorists. They are actually a help, finding cultural heritage in cultivated fields where farming activities might have ruined it forever. In rarer cases, they even discover areas that hadn't previously been considered archaeologically important..."

"OK!" Etta cut her off unceremoniously. She was getting a

little bored with the virtues of the Danish system. "But what if, despite all this fairness, someone was desperate to sell some jewels, or perhaps a conspicuous number of golden coins, to someone on the island and strike a deal? Who would they go to?"

The woman considered the question. "No, I really cannot think of anybody. Actually, I'd say the whole scheme was absurd. Consider how tightly knit our community is. No one would ever think..."

Etta snorted. She could not believe people on Ærø were any different to the rest of the world. *Come on, even back home in Castelmezzano, a village of 800 souls, we've got the good and the bad. Possibly more of the good, there's more social control, but I will never believe in a utopian island of saints.* But for once, she only voiced some of her thoughts.

"We shouldn't forget that someone on the island killed a person and hid the body."

"That's true," the woman said, slouching in dismay. "But I can't think of anyone."

"Maybe you could help us in establishing what of value could have been found?"

"I guess you mean commercial value?"

"That's right."

The woman turned her back on Etta to search through a file on the bookshelves behind her desk.

"Recently, some Viking treasure was found on an island on the northern side of Fyn. It might mean nothing. But ever since, many of us have harboured a hope that we would find real treasure on Ærø, too."

As Etta browsed through the article the director had handed her, she saw golden coins with a clear cross design, along with an earrings and pendant set, the gold markings forming spiral patterns that somehow made the jewellery look more modern than ancient.

"Art is timeless," Dora said in awe.

Never had she been so right.

~

It was late afternoon and Dora was still looking at the market stalls, enchanted by the Christmas decorations on sale. She had made a long list of names, people in Castelmezzano who would receive from her a little memento from Ærø.

"Dorotea Rosa Pepe, if we spend all our money at the Christmas market, not one of your presents will make it back home, for the simple reason we won't be able to pay for the petrol!"

"But Etta, dear, I'm only going for small things, like these decorated jars. Once we're back home, I will cook some Danish biscuits and fill them. As for the rest, I'm just daydreaming. It does you good, looking at pretty things."

Leon yawned. He'd had enough of people oohing and ahhing at him, asking to take a photo with him or petting him. Of course, celebrity comes at a high price, but he hadn't even met a pretty she-Basset yet!

"It's time to go and get a cup of coffee at the Aroma Café, just as Nathalie suggested." Quick as a flash, Etta slid her arm under Dora's and pulled her away from the stall, rather brusquely even by her standards.

"But Etta, I'm still choosing which..."

"Later."

"But we haven't tried the *gløgg* yet," Dora cried, dismayed. She had been looking forward to tasting the Danish version of mulled wine. But there was nothing she could do. She had to let go of her trove and allow herself to be dragged to the café. For once, though, even meek ever-patient Dora objected vociferously to the treatment. She sat sulkily in the café, rebelling by ordering a cappuccino this time, determined to make her feelings clear.

"What a strange setting," said Etta conversationally, looking around. "There are movie posters everywhere." In fact, there was barely a centimetre of wall without posters from the present and the past. They papered the whole place, including the counter. Even the long corridor leading to the toilets had a giant poster of Frank Zappa sitting on a WC, leaving no doubt as to where you were heading. Bookcases filled the space between the white-framed windows and a red sofa, a lamp giving the corner a cosy homely feeling. It was the kind of place that enticed you to sit down and pretend to read your book while you indulged in some people watching.

But Dora was in no mood for observation right now.

"I want to have one more look at the market stalls before they close."

"We can do that tomorrow, it's too cold for my taste."

"I thought you wanted to buy those felt slippers as a present for Auntie Clementina."

"I need to check her shoe size first."

Dora shook her head, failing to understand her friend's motivations. They'd been having such fun in the middle of the crowded market...

Then, through the window next to their table, she spotted a group of about 20 tourists following a man for an evening tour. And the guide was dressed up as a watchman.

"Oh, Etta!" Dora said, squeezing her friend's arm with barely contained affection and gratitude. "You wanted to make sure Leon didn't see him, just in case he reminded him of his previous owner." She didn't dare mention the name of the late Night Watchman of Rothenburg in case Leon overheard her.

"Once we're done with our coffee, we need to hurry back home and get ready for our dinner at Flemming's," said Etta, trying her best to look indifferent to her friend's words, but failing miserably when her eyes gazed down at the hound whose body was spread out on the red tiled floor, taking in all the warmth, his nose quivering at the nice smells of the café. Then she felt a squeeze in her heart, as if so much feeling could hardly be contained by such a little muscle. All she knew was that she didn't want this stubborn, confident, sweetest of doggies to suffer, even for a split second.

12

TOO OLD FOR LOVE

It was a pleasant evening at Flemming Grøn's house. The children were excited at having guests; they showed Etta and Dora their games room, the giant Christmas tree with real candles on, the letters to Santa they intended to send the very next day.

Flemming had prepared a simple but delicious dinner of *Frikadeller*, a Danish version of meatballs made with pork, served with a thick gravy, red cabbage and, of course, potatoes. He was very talkative when asked about his job at the local school, life on the island and how children on Ærø could experience a degree of freedom not easy to replicate elsewhere. He was vocal about the volunteer association he had joined which hosted workshops to teach children about the environment and preservation.

"Now," he said, after having scoffed one of the *Frikadeller* in his dish with gusto, "I have Emma and Thomas scolding me if I leave a light on when it's not necessary or run water when I'm brushing my teeth, but it's not only about increased awareness. They experience nature, life out doors. I know how important computers are, but I believe children should balance the digital world with plenty of time outside. They won't be respectful and care for the environment just because a bunch of stupid adults tells them to, but because they've experienced nature and feel a connection with it..."

His blue eyes were shining with the enthusiasm of sharing with his guests what he had learned. Every now and then, he would leave the table to pick up posters and slides the students at the association had prepared.

"So not only are you bringing up two children and teaching at the local school," Etta asked, bemused, "but in your spare time, you're working with children, too?"

"They're the future. And on a more selfish note, they keep me young. Emma says I'm an overgrown child..."

"That's true," said the girl. "Dad may look big, but he is just like us."

"But we take care of him," Thomas added, helping himself to one more scoop of the chocolate mousse Dora had prepared for them.

It was only when Thomas and Emma went to their room to play for the last thirty minutes before going to bed that Etta brought up the subject of the murder. She asked Flemming if he knew anything about it. He shook his head, seeming reluctant to get on to the subject. When Nathalie mentioned Sille and the fact that the police might think she was involved in the crime, Flemming fell so silent, it was impossible not to notice.

"What do you think?" Nathalie asked him curtly, determined not to give him a break, despite his distress.

"She's an adult, she can account for her behaviour."

Nathalie looked at him with a puzzled expression, but the man clearly didn't wish to elaborate on his statement and fell silent again.

"Can we help with the dishes?" asked Dora in an attempt to ease the tension in the room.

"Oh no, I will do that," said Nathalie.

"I believe you promised to read to Thomas and Emma," Dora replied, looking at the clock on the wall.

"That's true."

"Not to worry, I'll do the dishes," said Flemming.

"And I'll send the children down to say goodnight, and join you again as soon as I've told them a bedtime story, then another and another as they seem more excited than ever today."

As Nathalie went to join the children, Etta stayed put in a nice armchair facing the Christmas tree, the glittering candles and the warm stove. Leon cuddled up beside her legs, determined to make the most of his pre-Christmas celebrations. But poor Flemming was not having such an easy time. An unusually determined Dora had followed him into the kitchen.

"I'M SURE NATHALIE LOVES THE CHILDREN." Flemming was red in the face, almost panting from the stress of discussing such a difficult and personal subject so openly. But he hadn't been able to convince this sweetest of ladies to move the conversation on to more neutral terrain.

"Don't you love her?" Dora replied amiably, determined to get to the truth.

"I... I..." This conversation was becoming Flemming's worst nightmare. "I do, of course I do... who could help loving her?"

"But?" she insisted relentlessly.

"But... but... but it's one thing for her to babysit the children for a couple of hours, or even a whole day; it's a different thing altogether to be a stepmother."

"Why?" Dora said, staring at him as if that wasn't enough and she was still waiting for the real explanation.

"Because..." now Flemming's face was as purple as the remainder of the red cabbage he was putting back in the fridge –

he had tried a couple of times to cover it with cling film, but after it had ended up all crumpled as his hands were so shaky and clumsy, he gave up and placed the bowl in the fridge as it was, "…because with two young children, I can't… I can't…" he was looking to the upper corners of the room as if he might find the right words on top of the kitchen cabinets.

"You can't what?"

The river finally burst its banks and a deluge of words flooded out of his mouth.

"I can't play at being a boyfriend. I'm a father first of all and that's a huge responsibility. It's fine when one's children are independent, ready to leave for university, but if I were to get engaged to a woman now – and frankly, I doubt Nathalie would say yes – she would have to take on the full package. It'd be much easier with a single mother my age. I'd become the stepfather of her children; we'd complete each other."

Flemming was dabbing sweat from his forehead and face, but he at least felt he had done his best to state his case, explain his position once and for all, and move on to a less emotional topic.

"I see," said Dora. The man sighed in relief. "Fortunately, though," she continued seamlessly, "life has a habit of not working out the way we plan. Nor, I believe, in the most logical way."

The man dropped the cloth he'd been using to wipe his face on the floor, his eyes looking at Dora in dismay. Had she not understood a single one of the painful words he'd said?

"You know," she continued as if nothing were amiss, "it's like a croupier dealing cards, you take it or leave it. You can't choose your cards, but you can play the game with the cards you're served."

"I didn't think you'd be familiar with card games." Flemming was still wondering why the discussion had taken such an unexpected turn and where the woman was heading.

"My father taught me quite a few lessons, he was a hardened gambler..."

"Did he win a lot?"

"Quite the opposite, he lost everything," said Dora, remembering the elegant home, the fine pieces of furniture that had been in the family for generations, all sold after her father's death to pacify a queue of creditors who turned up on her doorstep.

"Not a great teacher, then," said Fleming, still panting for air. It was as if the world he knew had disappeared and he was desperate for something familiar.

"That's not strictly true. You see, because he gambled so much, because he lost all his games, I believe he had a lot to teach... though in all honesty, I'm not sure he was aware of that."

"But didn't he leave you destitute?"

"I had my little job. He had his game, I had mine. And now I'm here, travelling with Etta and our dog, and I own half of a pretty house in Castelmezzano. Not that I had expected to be dealt a new hand this late in life, but as I said, you never know what the croupier is going to give you, or when. But it's never – never, ever – the cards you were expecting, so you do your best with what you're served."

"But you said you were a teacher. You cannot really think that Nathalie should give up her youth, her most carefree years, for me..."

"That's her hand of cards. You concentrate on your own!"

And with that, Dora picked up the cloth Flemming had dropped on the floor, hung it over the heater and headed for the living room.

13

A TRADITIONAL WINDMILL

"I have a lead," Nathalie whispered into the phone.

"Where are you?" Etta asked her, still sitting in front of her breakfast whilst Leon eyed her sourly. How dare the woman eat her meal and chat on the phone whilst a poor, dejected Basset Hound was waiting to go out for a long-overdue walk after a whole night in captivity?

"I'm in the office right now, covering the Sunday rota, but earlier this morning, I happened to be passing the police station when they were taking Malthe Gammelgaard in."

"Who is Malthe Gammelgaard?"

"He is an artist, lives near the Søby Windmill."

"I'm not exactly sure what you're saying."

"Well, I've often seen Malthe going to the pub. Sometimes, I've seen him in the local stores, not so often at the library. But I've never seen him being taken into the police station. And the area where he lives might not be an archaeological site, but it's close to Søbygård, the only castle we have on the island, and I'm sure I've seen a few detectorists there. I wondered if Agnieszka might have been searching close to his property."

"You mean that he might have seen her at the time and he has been called in by the police to give a witness statement?"

"Exactly." She paused meaningfully. "And in order to make sure, I went back to speak to Sille."

"Is her shop open on a Sunday?"

"Until Christmas, yes. You've seen how many tourists there are around."

"Carry on."

"I said I'd seen Malthe at the police station, and she confirmed that Agnieszka had told her she had been in the Søbygård area. Apparently, Agnieszka wasn't any more specific; she didn't mention the area near the mill, for example, which is further up from the castle, but I think we've found out enough."

"So should we go up there?"

"One of the attractions you don't want to miss on Ærø is the Søby Windmill. The path starts just in front of the Søbygård Museum, and from there you will find a signposted track to the mill."

"But we won't find traces of Agnieszka Kamiński two years after her disappearance."

"Hold on, I didn't say you would. Once you're at the windmill, what you will find is a nice farm. Malthe and his wife, Anne-Grethe, are artists, and they each have a gallery that is open to the public. They keep a few animals, too, as they are keen on organic products. So let's say you visit the windmill, you might end up going to see the art galleries, too. And it would only be polite to speak to the artists. Maybe they remember something."

"Well done!" Etta had to acknowledge she was impressed. Nathalie was a bright young woman and she was never touchy when Etta was a little brusque; they'd had a sort of understanding from the outset. Usually people tended to like Dora much more than Etta, not to mention Leon taking all the glory. To be fair, Etta had never been jealous about this; she had no desire to be considered an 'endearing creature', but that someone should like her, despite... despite, ahem... some little faults in her character... well, that came as a pleasant surprise to her. And if this liking came not from a daft old hag like her, but from a smart, lively young woman, that pleased her even more. If only Maddalena knew that her mother could be liked and trusted exactly as she was.

"Bugger off, Maddalena!" Etta uttered her familiar refrain. It wasn't the time to get lost on the rocky road of family relationships, and so she called out to Dora to announce their new plans for the day.

THE ROAD TO SØBY WAS JUST AS ENCHANTING AS THE rest of Ærø. They saw beautiful thatched cottages nestling amongst century-old oak and linden trees, fields resting for the winter, a little frost decorating the ochre soil, and the sea was never too far away. It was a cold morning, but the sun was shining: ideal conditions for a brisk walk.

Leon was sitting in the backseat of the Fiat 500. During their travels, he tended to lie down and sleep, but today, the new smells filtering into the car were too promising to resist. His nostrils were twitching with expectation. He loved exploring and felt his bipeds had made the right choice, sacrificing yet another museum visit for a drive out into the wilderness.

"Søbygård," said Dora, indicating the sign to the museum and castle. "There's the parking area."

They had a quick look at the white castle, which was actually more of a manor house, but with its own moat and drawbridge. It had a charm and character all of its own.

"We can come back later," said Dora, looking at her watch. "But we'd better reach the farm before lunchtime."

Etta nodded in agreement. They saw a path with white and

red signs climbing up a roundish little hill and they set the hound free. When they reached the top, they saw the path going down the other side, only to climb a higher hill in large steps cut into the grass. Down they went and up again. On this second hill, they could see the path going on, up and down a few more hills, and in the distance, sitting on the top of one of these hills, were the large blades of a traditional windmill.

Dora clasped her hands. Her fingers intertwined, her mouth opened, but she was unable to utter a cry because of the powerful emotions taking hold of her heart at the marvel before her. Etta sighed, wondering how long it would take her friend to come back to earth. Leon had done a few gallops up and down, chasing rabbits and squirrels and whatever other creature happened to cross the path of this born hunter. Now he woofed to prompt the two women to get a move on, but when he saw Dora, he too realised the softer of his bipeds was lost somewhere far beyond both Etta and him. It happened every now and then. All he had to do was to be patient (again!) and she'd return sooner or later.

But Etta was stiff and anxious. She was thinking yet again of Saint Teresa of Avila, whose expression on the Bernini sculpture in Rome was so much like Dora's in her ecstatic raptures. Should she make a remark about this? She decided to save time and breath and not voice her thoughts.

Very slowly, motion and speech returned to Dora. "Oh Etta, oh Leon, that's a real windmill. On this magical island, they've got it all, even a windmill. What more could you ask for? No matter where I am or how I get there, I will always remember being here, in this countryside on a hill between a castle, the sea, the forest and the fields, and the old windmill in the distance."

"And now, wouldn't it be nice to have a proper look at it?"

"Of course, let's go," and Dora moved on as if she'd never stopped. Leon barked in gratitude; his soft biped was back with the group and they could finally get going. Etta was relieved for exactly the same reasons.

They went through some hedgerows that formed a tunnel above their heads, and in the middle of the grove, they discovered a place where a message had been hidden in a section of bamboo cane. Etta felt excited, wondering if it might be something related to the Polish treasure hunter, but the yellowing pages were in Danish, complete with strange, colourful drawings.

"It must be a sort of treasure hunt," Dora said. "Maybe organised by Flemming's association or the like. The children must be delighted and thrilled to discover the clues."

Etta grumbled an answer.

Panting and sweating despite the chilly air, they finally climbed the last hill and stood at the foot of the Søby windmill. To their surprise, the windmill's main body was thatched. Dora had read in their guide that it had been built in 1881 as there was too much work for the older Vester windmill southeast of Søby. They had both been built by the Nissen family of millers.

"And that's all," Dora sighed. "I wish guides would give you more detail. What were the Nissen family members like? Who were their customers? What kind of grain did people take to the mills? What would they use the flour for? Tourist guide writers need a soupçon more imagination."

They sat on a bench. Dora had brought a thermos of fruit tea and honey with her, and it had never tasted so good. Happy to be rehydrated by something nice and warm, they were restored by the drink.

When they felt they had taken all the beauty and peace in – and this time, Etta was as enraptured as Dora – and when Leon had received a couple of snacks that Dora had baked for him and drunk fresh water from his travel bowl, then and then alone did they move a few steps past the mill. In a large field, they spotted, and were spotted by, two bay horses. Without further ado, the beautiful animals trotted from the far end of the field all the way up the hill, at times pretending to turn right or left, but they stopped only when they were facing the visitors.

"Even the horses on this island are friendly," said Dora, not believing her eyes. She pulled a little grass from beside her and handed it to them, not that grass was lacking in the horses' field, but they seemed to think her offering was the best ever.

She can charm horses, too, thought Etta, bewildered at the confidence of Dora, who was now patting the horses' necks with smooth movements. Etta had never liked pets, until Leon had somehow forced himself into her life, but the two horses were magnificent. She couldn't stop thinking how they had taken the trouble to come all the way up to them.

"Do you think I could stroke them, too?" she asked, uncharacteristically shyly.

"Of course, you can."

Etta lifted her hand clumsily towards the neck of one of the horses, feeling the strength and tenderness emanating from him. Sixty years and beyond, and still she had so much to learn from life.

"Hey, you two," a voice called from the field below. "Don't feed them any sugar."

"No, only grass," Dora cried. As they both felt it was the right thing to do, they followed the fence all the way down to get to know the horses' owner. After all, it seemed he was exactly the person they were looking for.

~

MALTHE GAMMELGAARD WAS A ROBUST MAN WITH A thick, scruffy beard. He looked much more of a farmer used to working outdoors than a refined artist, and his manner was extremely direct.

Ignoring Dora's polite "How are you?" he asked them curtly, "What do you want?"

"Your horses came over to greet us, they're really friendly."

"They are," he answered, without even casting a look at Leon who was expecting his customary share of greetings and compliments.

"At the tourist office, they said you have a gallery open to visitors." Dora didn't reveal that it had been Nathalie Strøm rather than a generic 'they' who had mentioned this. She thought the detail irrelevant at the moment.

"I have, come along." As he said this, he moved towards the farm and didn't say a single word more. Etta and Dora looked at each other; it'd be difficult to get this man to speak freely. Then Etta jerked her head towards Dora, pointing with her nose as if to say, "Your task is to try something else to get him talking."

They had reached the farm. A white building shaped like a horse's hoof, similar to a few they had seen on the road from Ærøskøbing to Søbygård, was topped by a thatched roof. In the courtyard, there were enough toys to show that at least a couple of children lived there. From a small window on the side, the delicious aroma of cooking food made its way towards them.

"Do you bake your own bread?" asked Dora.

"We do."

"You don't have an outside oven? In Italy, that's what we tend to use."

"We're thinking of building one, but at the moment, we use a small oven next to the kitchen stove."

"What kind of flour do you use here? Where we come from – Southern Italy – it's mainly durum wheat, but there are some varieties such as Senatore Cappelli that are much sought after."

"We use a mix of flours." For the first time, the man seemed almost interested. "And, of course, we like our traditional rye bread. Here, we actually produce our own rye flour."

"Is that an Ærø tradition?"

"I guess it's more of a Danish tradition."

"Are you from Ærø yourself?"

"No, my wife and I came to the island as it's a nice place for artists to live. There's enough tourists to keep our atelier going, houses are cheap, schools are good, and you get to have your privacy, too. Are you interested in paintings or photographs?"

Dora and Etta looked at each other, wondering what the right answer would be.

"Both, if it's possible."

"They're in separate ateliers – my wife is a photographer, I'm a painter." As he said this, he opened a door to a completely white room. The ceiling wasn't particularly high, but there was plenty of space on the walls for paintings. Before letting them inside, the man pointed to the opposite wing of the farm.

"I'll leave that door open for the photo exhibition. If you want to buy anything, there's a bell close to the main door. I need to finish my cooking – by the way, the dog is allowed in."

As the man stomped off after opening up the other atelier, Dora looked at Etta in dismay.

"I did my best to strike up a conversation with him, but it's like they say: the Danish don't go in for small talk."

"They're not going to sell much of their stuff, in that case," said Etta. "Just imagine if we were in Italy, the guy would have talked us to death about the inspiration behind his work, its meaning, how it came about. He'd have bored us to tears about the most important moments in his artistic career, but most of all, he wouldn't have left our side until we'd bought something."

"That's not the Danish way, I guess."

"Well, it sucks. He's not likely to see anyone else today, he could have been a tad more welcoming."

"We wouldn't have bought anything anyway," said Dora, looking at the price tags on the smaller paintings.

"In Italy, they would have had some smaller items on offer

for broke tourists like us, stripped the 'Made in China' labels off and passed them as their own."

"Here people trust each other. You're not supposed to cheat."

"Whatever. But he's making our sleuthing even more difficult than it already was."

They left the first gallery and entered the second one. It was very similar, but here were photographic portraits and a few landscapes of places they hadn't yet seen on the island. Some small details had been blown up into large images, and they all used the same soft light and gentle colours, a delicacy and attention to detail. The woman's photography was in stark contrast to her husband's harsh manners.

"As we're not buying anything, are we supposed to leave without even saying goodbye?" said Etta when they had finished their tour of the galleries.

Dora nodded; the man had been quite clear that they should only ring the bell to make a purchase. But when they were in the courtyard again, Etta moved directly to the main door and clanged the bell aggressively.

"We'll try the Viking way this time."

14

DANISH BREAD AND BUTTER

Malthe Gammelgaard appeared on the threshold. He didn't say a word, nor did he ask them if they liked what they had seen. Instead, he waited for the two women to reveal why they had called him.

"We need to ask you a few questions," said Etta. "I'll be as brief as possible. We're staying at Freja and Magnus Holm's house back in Ærøskøbing, and a strange series of circumstances led us to find the corpse of a Polish woman in their attic. Did you hear about that?"

The man nodded. Even he, the insular artist, had heard the shocking news.

"The police mentioned," Etta stretched the truth a little here, implying that the police were sharing information with them, "that on the last day Agnieszka Kamiński was seen alive, she was doing some metal detecting in this area, and that you saw her."

The man didn't stir an inch, his face remaining impassive. Etta realised she should have made her question even more explicit.

"When did you see her? What did she tell you about her finds?"

To Etta and Dora's surprise, the straight question elicited a straight answer.

"I saw her on two consecutive days. We didn't speak the first time, she was on the other side of the mill," and he indicated upwards to the area on the left of the mill, the opposite direction to which Dora and Etta had arrived. "The next day, I saw her again, almost in same area, but this time in the middle of a field. I was out with my dog. I asked her if she had found anything..."

"You asked her?" said Etta in surprise.

"I did. I had been observing her unseen for a while, and her metal detector had been in a frenzy. It seemed she was finding one thing after another. She'd just take the time to clean the earth from each discovery, pass over it with another instrument, and then she'd put it in a little pouch. Then she'd move on to the next. It was one after the other, so I knew she was on to something. Normally, a detectorist will find something every thirty minutes or so on a good day; they might be lucky enough to find a few more pieces close to each other, but not that many."

"So that's why you spoke to her?"

"Yes. She was startled; with her ear defenders on, she had not heard me coming. But then she said she'd found a few old buttons and nothing more. She actually showed me a box full of them, all rotten with no discernible pattern at all. They could have been ancient or modern, beyond recognisable, and even antiques in that condition would have had no great value."

"But you mentioned a pouch, not a box," said Etta.

For the first time, the man smiled at her. "Well spotted! I'm sure she was using a pouch for her findings, but all she showed me was a box full of useless buttons."

"And what did you do?"

"I informed her that in Denmark, troves should be handed in to the local museum, who will report the finding to the National Museum. I also reminded her that detectorists who help the authorities are paid a fair price for their findings."

"And what did she say?"

"She shook her head and said that it wouldn't be worth the hassle, and that she intended to leave the buttons where she had found them. She also offered to hand them over to me."

"Did you take up the offer?"

"Of course not."

"You're not a treasure hunter yourself?"

"I'm not."

"But you seem well informed."

He chuckled and his straight face softened, looking more mischievous than the women would ever have imagined.

"With the school, my children were taken out treasure hunting and taught the importance of handing back the trove to the whole community. Of course, once back home, the children taught us parents what they'd learnt at school."

"What a great system, the school educating the children, and the children passing it on to their families," Dora said, clasping her hands. She'd always believed that even the most stubborn, belligerent adults would listen to their kids. "It's the same in Castelmezzano and Pietrapertosa, our home villages. When they started the recycling programme, the municipality had poor results. But when the significance of the programme was taught in the schools, the children became real ecowarriors, teaching their parents and relatives why it was so important to recycle and how they should go about it. In under three months, we'd hit our recycling quota, whereas in the previous year, we'd barely managed 15 per cent."

"Wait a second." The man went back inside, only to emerge moments later followed by a blonde woman with alabaster skin and a serious expression on her face, looking as if butter wouldn't melt in her mouth.

"This is Anne-Grethe, my wife. When I told her you're from Italy and believe in the role of children in changing society, she was eager to meet you, too. We'd love to talk to you some more and were wondering if you might want to stay for lunch. Your dog, too. Just broth and bread, though, maybe a little more but no lasagne nor spaghetti Bolognese, I'm afraid."

Etta and Dora promptly took up the offer, exchanging stunned glances. This man, who had hardly deigned to say a word to them earlier, was now inviting them to join something as intimate as the family Sunday lunch. For his part, Leon was confused by the fact the husband and wife had failed to see what a great honour had been bestowed on their humble abode with the visit of such a worthy Basset. The three visitors, although via different paths, came to the same conclusion at the same time: the Danish were mysterious creatures, indeed.

They entered a living room that was so warm, it was almost too hot. A large tree stood in pride of place, decorated with real candles. Two children came forward to introduce themselves to the visitors, but once they spotted Leon, all their attention was on him. They gently patted him, fired at least ten questions each at the two adults escorting him, begged their parents to let them have such an adorable dog too, and Leon finally felt that equilibrium had at least partially been restored.

"We only light the tree candles in the evening and on weekends," Anne-Grethe explained, "as during the working day, they might be left unattended. But we can light the first candle of Advent together now." So saying, the woman placed a centrepiece decorated with fir branches and pine cones on the table and invited the children to do the honours.

"Next Sunday, we will light the second candle, and by Christmas, they will all be lit," the older boy explained.

Spreading exquisite creamy butter on her rye bread, which

was still warm from the oven – a delicious companion to the vegetable broth, Dora asked how they made it taste so good.

"My neighbour and I make the butter," Anne-Grethe explained, her face softening into what almost resembled a smile. "Industrial butter is often made from the remains of the cheese production cycle, but this butter is made out of crème fraiche, the richest part of the milk. That is why it is so creamy and tasty. We also use a pinch of salt."

For the main course, the diners enjoyed pork with roast potatoes and a little cabbage salad. The younger child prepared a bowl for Leon, a few pieces of meat and potatoes, a dish the dog found so tasty that he could almost forgive the grown-up Danes for ignoring him. Dessert was a cake made with plums.

Once the dinner was done and the children had asked if they could go out and play with Leon, talk turned to life on the island.

"Do you happen to know Sille Skytte of the Ærøskøbing Antiques shop?" Etta asked Malthe, implying the question was inherent to what they were talking about.

"Of course we do. You see, we all get to know each other on the island."

I wonder how you get to know each other, when you're so disinclined to talk, Etta thought, but the man evidently didn't feel any need to elaborate on the information he had just provided, obliging her to formulate a more specific question.

"Do you work with her? Maybe you sell your paintings in her shop?"

"Yes, that has happened a few times. She stocks some of my more classic pieces, and once a month, I visit her to see if she's sold any."

Silence fell. Unexpectedly, it was the hostess who came to the rescue.

"Is it correct that you drove all the way to Denmark in a Fiat 500?" asked Anne-Grethe incredulously.

"We did once have a very nice, practical saloon," replied Etta. "But *someone* wouldn't get rid of her car, so I was forced to give up my creature comforts."

"The good thing is," Dora added, "that in such an old car, you can't drive too fast so we won't get a single speeding fine. And it's been a good runner for so many years..."

Etta, forthright as ever, couldn't help asking Malthe why he had all but ignored them in the beginning, and then decided to invite them for lunch.

"I'm afraid we are not too keen on small talk," Malthe explained. "We're aware this might put some people off, but I don't want to comment on the weather. That's such a waste of time when I can just go online and find out all I need to know."

"But people can't go straight into discussing Schopenhauer or nuclear physics. Small talk is a useful way to start a conversation, then you can move it on to something more meaningful when you find you have something in common."

"But to save us time..."

"Pardon me, but it doesn't seem you're as rushed up here as the folks in Copenhagen."

"But we value time with our family and friends," Anne-Grethe justified. "If we were to talk about the weather with all the tourists who pass by, a good chunk of that time would be gone."

"And what's the purpose?" After lunch, Malthe had filled a pipe with tobacco, but he hadn't lit it; instead, he kept moving it in and out of his mouth. "Those people will go back to their countries and families, and we won't ever get a chance to speak to them again."

"Danish people take friendship very seriously," Anne-Grethe went on explaining. "We might not be concerned about talking to strangers, but friendship in our world is meant to last forever."

"What about the passenger on the train?" asked Dora.

"The *what?*"

"The chance encounter with a total stranger on the train where you will confide in him or her more than you've ever confided to your closest friend or spouse."

"Good grief!" cried Anne-Grethe. "Why would you ever do that?"

"Because you will never meet her or him again, so there will be no repercussions!"

"Well, if someone tried to confide in me on a train, I'd think they were a sex maniac or a serial killer, or – and this is best-case scenario – they didn't have all their marbles in the right place. I wouldn't want to speak to them, that's for sure."

"But a good chunk of world literature would be wiped out if no one spoke to each other on trains."

"Well, we know we don't always get it right, and that is why we invited you for lunch. We've decided to break out of our comfort zone at least once a month. It's really challenging for us, but maybe you're right and we could learn something."

"But no way am I going to invite every passing tourist to join us at our table," Malthe added, just to make sure the point was clear.

"You could find a happy medium," Dora laughed. "Maybe don't invite them all for lunch, but you could point out a few things of interest as you accompany them to your galleries."

"Never! That'd be far too smarmy."

Etta banged her forehead with her right hand. "You might want to spend a year in Italy, see how things work somewhere else," she said, and Dora added a couple of examples of what smarmy really meant in their country. "So after a trip to Italy, you could strike the perfect balance between the two extremes," Etta concluded, as the others chuckled.

"What do you think?" asked Etta, her head a little fuzzy because of the beer she'd been drinking – luckily, she had refused the Schnapps. "Not at my age," she'd said. Dora had refused all alcohol as she was driving back; she didn't feel comfortable driving on the main roads, but the Danish country lanes, perfectly smooth and not too narrow, were relaxing for her.

"I don't think they've got anything to do with the murder, otherwise Malthe would not have been so open about his conversation with the Polish detectorist."

"Yes," Etta mulled over her friend's words, "or he could simply have told us about the useless buttons and not even mentioned the hidden pouch."

"So it seems you were right, Agnieszka really did find something of value."

"I believe whatever she found is the lead we should follow. Agnieszka must have approached someone – probably her killer – in town and tried to strike up a deal with him or her, but then the killer must have thought it was more convenient to get rid of her altogether and keep the trove for themselves, which again leads me to think that it must have been valuable."

"Which was why," Dora completed her thoughts, "she only revealed her useless findings to Malthe."

"It's exactly the same technique truffle hunters use in Castelmezzano. If hikers approach them in the forest, they only show the most miserable things they've found to discourage other folks from searching in a promising area."

~

Dora kept driving, and Etta kept watching, thinking and discussing, brooding and musing. And the fellow in the backseat? He was happy to rest his weary paws. They had decided to follow Anne-Grethe's advice to drive slowly – oh so slowly – the extra six kilometres that would take them through the village of Søby to the Skjoldnæs Fyr, the lighthouse on the most north-western tip of the island.

Dora parked the car and they took a little path through the fields. The grass was so luscious, it covered the hilly terrain of the golf course around the pinkish stone lighthouse like a luxurious carpet. There was no one around, but at night-time, they read on a sign, the Skjoldnæs Fyr sent its beacon over the waters, still guarding the safety of ships and sailors.

Normally open to visitors, the lighthouse was closed this late on a wintry afternoon. It didn't matter to the two women; they could always come back, but this moment was precious. From the tip of the tongue of land, suspended above the rocks, they admired the panorama over the sea on all sides. As the glorious light of the sunset wrapped everything in its golden blanket, even Etta stood still in contemplation just like Dora. Only Leon remained unmoved, wondering if Dora's disease was contagious, and was he at risk too?

Like the loyal and brave guard dog he was, Leon stood beside his bipeds to make sure they wouldn't tumble down into the sea in their trance. But when he saw them coming back to their senses, he couldn't resist any longer. The breeze, the damp grass, the seagulls crying in the distance, the rabbits he imagined running in front of him – it was all too much and he started to rush about in mad gallops. Dora and Etta, laughing at his antics, secretly wished they could do just the same. Instead, they kept walking, hungry for more views, the peaceful sea below them looking like a lake so vast, it was impossible to see the other shore. And for long, blissful moments, the murder, the victim, the suspects, the killer were all forgotten.

15

A TOWN OF SAILORS AND PIRATES

On Sunday evening, Nathalie had messaged Etta and asked if she could see them after dinner. They'd held a real conspirators' meeting: low lights, candles at the window, hot cup of tea and a few *bruncager*, the butter, pistachio and spice Christmas biscuits from the local bakery. Etta and Dora had updated her on their findings, making Nathalie more excited than ever at the thought of real treasure being found on Ærø.

"But it must be long gone," she said, second thoughts tempering her enthusiasm. "The murderer must have found a way to dispose of it; he must have known who to get in touch with on the mainland – people who had the know-how to smuggle things wherever they wanted. But if we find the killer, we might still be able to track the treasure and have it returned to the island."

"Maybe," said Etta, doubtfully.

"Certainly!" said Dora at the same time.

Nathalie had done her fair share of sleuthing, discovering that Camilla Egede, the occupant of the first-floor flat at the time of the murder, still lived on Ærø, but had moved to Marstal in the northern part of the island. A colleague at the Tourist

Information office actually knew her and had given Nathalie Camilla's contact details. The young woman had then phoned Camilla and asked if she could arrange a meeting over a cup of coffee for two Italian ladies who were on the island, researching local arts and crafts.

So now, on Monday morning, Etta, Dora and Leon were driving the 13 kilometres from Ærøskøbing to Marstal. They'd enjoy a day of tourist attractions, and later in the afternoon, as soon as she'd finished work, Nathalie would meet them and they'd all go to visit Camilla.

It was a cold, misty morning, and the island looked rather different to when it was bathed in winter sunshine. Nonetheless, Dora kept clasping her hands during the drive, exclaiming now at the beauty of steamy fields gently sloping down towards the sea, now at the numerous farms that, even in the barren winter, oozed the charm of olden times. Etta, relaxed as there was no traffic on the Ærø roads, had to agree that the drive was rather scenic and one to be remembered. Not that she approved of Dora's dramatic ways. She even had to scold her friend when Dora opened her window in order to take it all in, chilly air from the sea included.

Their first stop was the Maritime Museum, dramatically announced as such by the stern of a ship sticking out of the building as if it had leapt from the sea and ploughed through it by mistake. A pirate stood next to the entrance, his threatening glare driving Napoleon to growl menacingly until Dora placed the two next to each other, adjusted the dog's Danish flag bandana and asked him to smile. Leon did not smile; instead, his nose subjected the crooked man to a thorough investigation until he realised the pirate was made of plastic and he could finally relax. But Dora, of course, was quite happy with the shot of Leon nosing the suspicious figure.

The two friends were ready to take it in turns to visit the museum, but a softly spoken lady, so thin that Etta feared speaking a little louder would blow her away, had different ideas.

"I'd say that fellow looks like an intelligent dog, and there's not a single visitor here today..." she leant over the counter on her elbows as if she was ready to whisper a secret no one else should hear, "and the director is away in Copenhagen..."

"And?" asked Etta when the woman looked meaningfully at them.

"Then, I'd say..." the woman looked around to make sure no one was hiding behind the walls.

"My goodness, spit it out!"

The woman winked at Etta. "You can go in with your dog. If someone else turns up, I will ask them if they have a problem with that."

"You mean you'll allow Leon in?"

The woman nodded with so much energy, Etta now feared her small neck might break, her head rolling across the floor away from her body. But it stayed where it belonged as she issued two tickets.

"I had understood Danish people always followed the rules," Etta couldn't resist speaking her mind. "They'll never even cross the road when the crossing light is at red, even if there's no car around for miles..."

The woman smiled, lowering her head as if to acknowledge such foibles existed. Then she leant so far over the counter, her feet must have been hanging in the air on the other side as she whispered her latest revelation.

"I'm descended from a family of pirates."

"I see," Etta said. "I suspected something of the sort."

"We pirates make Denmark more fun."

"That's true!"

"But you better get going before some common sailor comes along and spoils everything."

The Maritime museum was intriguing for the variety of its

collections, ranging from a full wall display of model ships in bottles, to ancient and modern art depicting life at sea. And in a Danish version of *National Geographic,* the incredibly clear paintings by JEC Rasmussen revealed the dramatic landscapes of Greenland and its people.

Dora was attracted by a number of figureheads depicting women dressed in white with a blue band around their waists, making them look like female sailors. Etta's attention was drawn to a collection of letters – nicely translated into English, too – from sailors to their families waiting for them on land. They described life onboard and how they hoped to return home soon. Leon eyed a shrunken head suspiciously, while Dora simply wouldn't look at it. Etta said there were quite a few people she knew whose heads she would have liked to see in brine.

"They're mentioned in the book *We, the Drowned* by Carsten Jensen," was all Dora would say. "It tells the stories of sailors' families from Marstal along the centuries."

When the visit was finally over, Etta asked the woman at the counter if she could recommend somewhere for refreshments.

"Do you want a tourist place or a pirate place?"

"Pirate, of course," said Etta. And the woman gave them directions to somewhere not too far from the museum on the left, where they'd still be close to the sea.

When they entered the smoky room, where they could hardly make out the faces of the quirky characters within, Dora and Etta looked at each other, wondering if a tourist place might not have been a better choice. They were standing on the threshold, tempted to turn on their heels and leave, when Leon pulled them forward, as enthusiastic as ever. A man saw them from behind the bar and signalled to the two women to choose which table they preferred, and he'd come and take their order.

Leon marched towards the innermost table. Etta, choking on the smoke, followed him and took a seat.

"I wonder," she said between one cough and the next, "if he likes this dingy place because it reminds him of The Devil's Ale." Leon's former owner, Sebastian Sauer, used to be a regular in that pub where all the rogues and scoundrels of Rothenburg ob der Tauber would gather.

"Maybe, just like there, the people here are not as bad as they look," Dora suggested.

"They certainly smell as bad as they look," replied Etta, unconvinced. The combination of tobacco, alcohol and too little ventilation for so many people was overwhelming. But the really eerie thing was the quiet. Some of the pirates were speaking, but their voices were surprisingly muffled. Maybe there was some music playing, but if it was, the volume was so low, it was lost in the murmurs.

The waiter from the bar came over to them with a menu that consisted of only one page. As it was in Danish, the only word the women recognised was *smørrebrød*, which was just the type of food they wanted at that time of day. Not overly hungry, they needed a little sustenance after the visit to the museum and before discovering the rest of the maritime town.

"No Schnapps?" the man asked, eyeing them suspiciously.

"No Schnapps," replied Dora, horrified. She had never in her entire life drunk alcohol at 11am. "Actually, a tea for me, please."

Etta asked for a cappuccino. And the man looked at her in shock.

"That frothy stuff with milk?" He evidently thought the drink to be harmful to the health system.

"Indeed."

"Nope, sorry, a white coffee is the closest I can get."

"A white coffee then." As the man left the table, Etta whispered, "You know, maybe it isn't so bad we ended up here. I wonder if our Polish friend ever came this far in her search for a deal. From what we read in the museum, it seems that Marstal is the town of sailors, ships and trade… she might have found some contacts here. And of all places in the town she would have tried, this is a likely candidate."

As usual when Etta's brain was working this fast and suggesting the most improbable connections, Dora struggled to keep up. In the past few months, she'd learned that her friend had a real flair for investigations, and she unquestioningly trusted Etta's instincts.

"And nothing happens just by chance," she commented. "Maybe there is a reason why we're here."

The man came back with a large bowl full of water. The hound sniffed at it in disgust and fixed two melancholy eyes on him, as if saying, "Is this the best you can offer to a poor, starving dog?"

"Hey, pal, I don't think those two ladies will allow me to serve you a Schnapps."

Etta's eyebrows shot up well above the large frames of her glasses. "Of course not."

"And I don't have any cappuccino, either," the man said as the dog's expression turned to bleak despair, "but I'll be back."

The man returned minutes later with three plates of *smørrebrød,* placing one down in front of Leon. For maximum effect, the dog made a mournful face as if the two women hadn't fed him for the last couple of months. For her part, Etta got her coffee with two pots of cream.

That must be the closest thing they have to milk, she thought. But to her and Dora's surprise, the *smørrebrød* were colourful, tasty and laid out with an unexpectedly keen eye for aesthetics.

"They look marvellous," said Dora appreciatively. The man smiled, but his eyes were glued on Leon.

"The poor dog has eaten very little these past few days," lied Etta. Dora was going to protest, but a kick on her shin turned her protest into a cry of despair for the 'poor dog'.

"How come?" asked the man.

"Maybe you've heard the news?"

The man shook his head.

"A few days ago, in the attic of the house we're staying in, my dog and I found the remains of that poor Polish woman who disappeared on the island a couple of years ago."

"I see what you mean now," the man cried. "Yes, I heard the latest news on the radio this morning. The police have confirmed that the body discovered on Friday is that of the Polish detectorist."

Etta raised her eyebrows and gave Dora a meaningful glance. Up until now, they had been assuming the skeleton belonged to Agnieszka Kamiński; now they knew for sure.

"Was it really this clever Basset who found her?" the waiter continued. "This chap's amazing."

Etta wondered why, whenever you say "My dog and I", most people only hear "My dog". She then decided it would be a good idea to leverage Leon's charms to get more information before the man recovered from the spell.

"Yes, we don't know what he sensed, but he kept pointing at the wall and whining and scratching." A little dramatisation would only enhance the tale. "In the end, we had to find out what was behind it. The dog has been too distressed to eat ever since."

"That poor lass," said the man.

"Did you ever meet her? Or did she just stay put in Ærøskøbing?"

"Oh no, she was in Marstal, too," the man said with pride, confirming that the ancient rivalry between the two towns was still alive. "She sat at this very bar one evening."

"Did she?"

"Sure."

"And was she alone?"

"No, she was speaking to Villads Grøn and another man I'd never seen before."

"Who is Villads Grøn?"

"He was a sailor."

"Was? Has he retired?"

"Nope, one night, a couple of months after the woman disappeared, he got drunk and plunged into the sea."

"Plunged?"

"Yes, it seems he tried to climb on some boats in the harbour, lost his balance and down into the cold water he went. He'd never have managed to swim ashore quickly enough, the state he was in."

"My goodness!" cried Dora.

"And did the police interview him at the time of the woman's disappearance?"

"I think so. The police asked all of us who had seen the woman to come forward, but Villads was never thought to be involved in her disappearance. He wasn't the kind of man who was interested in long-lost treasures."

"Do you remember what the other man looked like?"

"He was a sailor, tall chap, thick black beard. He didn't speak much."

"Did you see him again?"

The man seemed surprised by the question; he took some moments to think it over.

"Well, no, now you come to ask, I never did see him again, neither in my pub, nor in town."

16

ONE WOMAN'S MEAT IS ANOTHER WOMAN'S POISON

When they left the pub, they took a little tour of Marstal with Dora naming a few places and reminding herself of Carsten Jensen's book. Unlike Ærøskøbing, Marstal was undulating, but it seemed all its streets eventually led down to the harbour, which was pretty much the heart and soul of the town. There were possibly fewer shops than in Ærøskøbing, but their decorations were just as pretty and the two women promised themselves they'd return at the weekend when the Christmas market would be in full swing.

Marstal had the same colourful beach cabins as Ærøskøbing, including the only cabin with a thatched roof on the whole island. This also boasted red walls, green door, white framed windows and the ubiquitous Danish flag waving from a pole. It was possibly more photographed by tourists, whether they be romantic couples, young families, sulky hubbies and nagging wives, or lone travellers, than any other place on Ærø. And Dora, of course, wanted not only to see it, but also to have a shot taken with Leon wearing his Danish bandana. Etta grumbled for a while, but more because that was expected of her than because she really felt sulky. Which she didn't. In fact, now that the sky had cleared a bit, she was enjoying standing on the tongue of land called Erikshale that acted as a protective arm, almost enclosing a large portion of the sea as if it were a lake and separating it from the wilder open waters that lay to the south. Calm water on one side, stormy wildness on the other. That's how Etta felt so often, pretending – which is not the same as achieving – an outward appearance of calm while feeling *Wuthering Heights* inside…

They stopped to talk with a lady walking a little poodle. As the poodle was a she-dog, Leon instantly turned into her slave. She bit his ears, invited him to gallop, then demanded they play throw and catch – which he never usually did. Of course, he let her win when they raced after the ball.

Males are hopeless, no matter the breed and species, Etta thought.

The woman offered to take a photo of the three of them next to the red cabin with the thatched roof. And Dora was simply enthralled: they had the very shot that a million tourists had taken before them. But Etta had to agree that Leon looked gorgeous, as usual, and even she and Dora offered some variety of the human kind to the much photographed landmark.

Just before four o'clock, as the sun was setting, Nathalie joined Dora and Etta in the car park, having got a lift with a colleague who lived in Marstal. On the road between Marstal and Standby, Nathalie asked Etta to stop at a pretty white cottage. Despite the incoming darkness, they could still distinguish the silver birches around the house and the little white fence enclosing what would be a pretty garden in summer. The glittering waters of the sea were visible at the back of the house – on Ærø, the sea was never too far away.

They had reached Camilla Egede's home.

~

CAMILLA OPENED THE DOOR. SHE WAS OLDER THAN

Nathalie, but still a young woman by Etta and Dora's standards, possibly in her early thirties.

"Hello," she said, a small smile on her thin pink lips. She had dark brown hair and deep slate-grey eyes topped by two long brows that resembled the wings of a seagull in full fight over the sea. Nathalie and she exchanged a few words in Danish, and then Camilla led them all into the living room, their footsteps echoing in the empty house. There was furniture, but all the personal things that make a house feel cosy – books, pictures, paintings, even the stupid things we buy on impulse, then never know what to do with when we return home – were missing.

Etta looked around and saw a number of boxes beyond the sofa.

"Are you just moving in?"

Camilla chuckled. "No, I'm moving out."

"A new home?" asked Nathalie.

"And possibly a new life, too. I'm leaving the island."

"You're leaving Ærø?" repeated Nathalie. According to her, no one in their right mind would leave the idyllic island of their own volition.

"It seems," Camilla laughed quietly, but her eyes were darting around nervously, "I've finally plucked up the courage..."

"But don't you love living here?"

"Not really, I feel like a prisoner. The funny thing is that I don't know what was holding me back."

"But why?" Nathalie insisted.

"An island is like a prison. You can't come and go as you please, you have to wait for a ferry to take you to the mainland, not to mention the times when the sea is rough and you're cut off from civilisation until the storm calms down."

"But that's exactly what makes it so cosy – it's a world apart. During the crossing, you feel like you're slowing down and entering a calmer way of life..."

"Oh, the crossings," Camilla said, shaking her head and looking at her feet, as if aware she was saying something that might not go down too well. "I despise those, too. Every one of the 75 minutes marks the fact you're getting further and further from the real world."

"Will you be going to Copenhagen?" Etta asked, marvelling at how different people's points of view could get. One of the fishermen they'd met on their first walk in Ærøskøbing had said that people on Ærø were so friendly and open because the sea *connected* the island to the rest of the world. This young woman saw that same sea as a symbol of isolation.

"Yes, I will stay in Copenhagen for a few months, only as long as is strictly necessary. I get fed up with city life easily, I need contact with nature."

"Will you be heading to Europe? Maybe Spain or Greece, somewhere close to the sea?" asked Dora.

"No, I'm not a fan of the Mediterranean. For so long, I've dreamed of living in Norway amongst the rugged mountains, going on serious hikes through the forest..."

"But you might be just as isolated there, despite not being on an island." Now it was Etta's turn to be puzzled.

"I know it sounds like a contradiction, but that's how I feel."

"Maybe Ærø is too tame for you?" said Dora.

Camilla laughed guiltily. "Too tame and too flat, I'm afraid. I long for real wilderness, but I need to stop in Copenhagen to study. I'd love to be able to teach online, and sell my products, too, but I need to upgrade my skills."

"Teach?"

"Not on a one-to-one basis. Nowadays you can create a course on any subject, upload it onto the internet, and someone will download it somewhere else in the world. I'm getting quite good at creating boiled wool and felt art, as well as making a few useful objects. I've run courses for tourists here on Ærø and I think they quite enjoyed it, but now I'm ready to take the next step. I've packed a lot of stuff, but I believe I still have something on hand to show you..."

Camilla left the living room and Etta walked around, though there was little to see, just a few notes scribbled on a pad next to her phone and a personal organiser. Making sure no one was watching, Etta opened the organiser and skipped through the pages. On the page for this very Monday, she read, *"Storage Unit Pris"*, a few incomprehensible Danish words, then *"København billet"* and finally *"Italienske kvinder"* – "the Italian women", clearly a reference to the meeting with her and Dora.

Camilla came back with a few things under her arm and a box that, despite being bulky, seemed light to carry. She showed them yoga mats, circular meditation rugs and some colourful felt objects they could hang on the walls instead of paintings.

"They are relaxing and help you avoid brooding."

As Dora and Nathalie were enthusiastic, Camilla opened the box she had carried in and showed them her collection of slippers, too.

"They're warm and light, and possibly my best sellers, though it's the abstract paintings I love the most."

"When did you decide to leave?" Etta asked.

Camilla blushed. "There wasn't a particular moment. I think the decision has been building in me gradually, even when I wasn't aware of it."

"But you must have decided on a date to move."

"I will join my family for Christmas. They live just outside Copenhagen, and I might use their home as a base until I'm ready to leave for Norway."

"Why did you come to Ærø, of all places, if it is so far from what you like?"

"My ex-boyfriend, and I guess I was idealising island life. The truth is we face the same troubles here as anywhere else: we have unemployment, depression and problems with alcohol..."

"As do villages in Norway."

"I know, but I'm not expecting heaven on earth this time. I know what it's going to be like."

"And your ex-boyfriend?"

"He's found a new girlfriend. They're getting married soon, but truly, there are no hard feelings on my side. Not that I'm happy, either; it's never pleasant to find yourself alone, I can't deny that, but that's life, isn't it? We might believe we've found 'the one', and then we discover how wrong we were... but I wasn't expecting to be discussing my private life with you this afternoon. I thought you were interested in my artwork."

This time, it was Nathalie who blushed – she'd been the one to give that impression to Camilla – but Dora had it covered.

"I'm sorry. We're on the island temporarily and we do like to see the local artwork, but it's good to stumble on human stories, too, and discover the whole world is not too different from place to place." And she told Camilla about her nephew, the talented but hapless Arturo, who was trying to set up a new business in Bari, almost three hours away from home, after having been unsuccessful wherever he'd been before.

"Is he an artist?"

"In a way," Dora said, whilst Etta looked at her in wonder. To the more pragmatic woman, Arturo was nothing but a rascal trying to make easy money one way or another, and that included extorting it from his generous auntie with a different pitiful story each time they met. "But he still lacks enough confidence in himself to let his artistic side express itself freely."

Etta felt it was her moral duty to interrupt the conversation.

"By the way, I'm sure you've heard about the skeleton of poor Agnieszka Kamiński being found?"

"Sure, I've heard about that," but Camilla was clearly startled by the abrupt change of subject.

17

CONJECTURE

"Did you realise Agnieszka – well, what was left of her, anyway – was found in the attic above your former flat?" Etta asked Camilla.

"Oh gosh! I didn't realise it was there."

"You don't watch the news?"

"Not really," said Camilla, indicating the lack of a TV in the empty room.

"You already packed it?"

"No, I prefer not to have one. And I prefer not to follow the news, neither on the radio nor online. I heard people talking about the body being found, remembered the time when the woman disappeared, though I can't see how she happened to end up in the attic above my flat. What was her connection with the Holms?"

"The connection might not have been with the Holms as they were away at the time. But Sille Skytte was renting the attic. Do you remember anything peculiar happening around that time?"

Camilla paused. "What do you mean?"

Is she trying to buy time?

"Someone must have taken Agnieszka up to that attic, dead or alive. She'd been seen at the local pub the day before her disappearance, then two years later, her remains are found in the attic above where you were living at the time. I was hoping someone may have seen her after she left the pub."

"I see what you mean. I can't say I remember what happened that day – it's two years ago now, but I'm sure there was nothing that caused me to think Agnieszka's disappearance had anything to do with the Holms' house and the people who used it. So I can safely say that no, I didn't notice anything peculiar or strange. I certainly didn't see Agnieszka walking past my flat."

"So you don't have any specific memories of that day?"

"Don't tell me you can remember what you did on 29 October two years ago, or 5 November last year, or..."

"No, I can't," Etta cut short what was shaping up to be a lecture on how easy it is to forget what one has done even the day before, "unless there's a good reason to remember."

"As I said, nothing stands out for me. I remember when the alarm was raised after her friends realised she had disappeared – of course I remember that because nothing ever usually happens on Ærø, but I didn't connect that with the place I was living..."

"Did you ever meet Agnieszka?"

"Yes. Her picture was all over the news – even I couldn't help but notice – and I realised I had seen her coming back into town with her metal detector equipment. And I saw her at the Aroma Café. We exchanged a few words. You know how easy it is for two lone women to get chatting, but it doesn't necessarily lead to anything interesting."

"So you spoke to her?"

"Yes, sometime in the middle of her week here. I even went to the police when they asked anyone who had seen the woman to come forward."

"And what did they say?"

She laughed. "They were just as inquisitive as you are. And I told them that she had told me about her searches and asked if I was interested in ancient artefacts."

"And what did you say?"

Camilla hesitated yet again. "Of course I like them, I admire the design of the things I have seen in museums. She told me she was hoping to find something interesting on the island... and that was that."

"She didn't show you anything?"

"No."

"Did she say she'd found something of value?"

Camilla shook her head.

"She didn't ask for your help in finding a buyer for her trove?"

"Not at all," the woman replied firmly. But Etta wasn't convinced she was telling the truth. When Dora bought some of Camilla's slippers and insisted that one of the round rugs would be perfect for Leon, Etta was so thoughtful, she didn't reply as she usually would that they should be more careful with their money or they would have to either hitchhike home or crowdfund every litre of petrol they put into the car.

BACK IN THE CAR, NATHALIE WAS IMPATIENT TO KNOW Etta's impressions of Camilla. First, though, Etta updated her on what the bartender had told them about the sailor named Villads Grøn who had been seen speaking to Agnieszka.

"Is he related to Flemming, by any chance? Or is Grøn just a common Danish surname?"

"I've heard the children referring to Granddad Villads, and I know he worked in Marstal." Nathalie gave the matter some thought. "I believe he had a drink problem, and that he passed away two years ago, drowned in the harbour. Too many coincidences, it must be the same man."

Again, thought Etta, *the murder has a connection to Flemming Grøn and his family. First his mother-in-law, now his father, despite Nathalie wishing to deflect suspicion away from the man she loves.* It didn't come as a surprise when the young woman took the conversation in a different direction.

"And how about Camilla?" she asked, reiterating her original question. "What do you think of her?"

"I have a feeling she's not telling us the whole truth. She's hiding something, but I wonder if it's just from us, or if she failed to speak the whole truth to the police, too."

"Do you believe that Agnieszka did actually ask her if she would be interested in buying some treasure? But Camilla's not rich, why approach her in the first place?"

"Let's assume you're Agnieszka, stuck with something of value that you'd rather not hand in to the authorities and a flight to catch shortly. You've spoken to the most promising buyer, Sille Skytte, and she's bluntly refused. There aren't any other antiques shops in Ærøskøbing, so when you happen to speak to Camilla, you may wonder whether to show her some of the artefacts you have found. After all, as an artist, she will be likely to recognise their integrity."

"And as she was so desperate to get away from Ærø," continued Nathalie, "the offer might have looked like a dream come true to Camilla. But if she murdered the detectorist in order to take the treasure, why didn't she disappear with the money right away? Why wait until now?"

"So as not to arouse suspicion. Or maybe, she did like the island after all and hoped the body would never be discovered."

"That'd be very silly of her."

"There's no law saying that murderers are geniuses… on the contrary. For sure, Camilla had easy access to the attic. Then there's her notes," and Etta told them what she had read in the organiser.

"What's wrong with that? She told us she was moving, and that she'd made the decision a few weeks ago..."

"Nope, she decided at the weekend. Possibly as soon as she heard the news that the remains had been found, otherwise she'd have enquired about the storage unit price some time back, the same for buying the ticket to Copenhagen. It's too much of a coincidence that she's doing it now. I'm sure it's a recent decision – she's running away."

Nathalie was unusually silent. It was only when they were arriving in Ærøskøbing that Dora asked her what she was thinking.

"Not about the murder, in truth, but about Camilla feeling like a prisoner on the island..."

"Are you afraid you, too, might be making the wrong choice on a whim? Camilla definitely has a different point of view of the island from everyone else."

"In a few weeks, when my internship finishes, I will go back to Copenhagen to complete my studies, but I'm planning to return to Ærø or at least try to get a job here. Camilla's made me realise that this choice is right for me. But in all frankness, I just can't understand her opinion at all. I've lived in New Zealand, Libya and Iran, Great Britain and more recently Copenhagen, and I don't think there's a perfect place for everyone. But I'm sure each of us has a perfect place, and mine, I know, is Ærø."

"You could change your mind later..."

"Then I'll have to deal with it."

"But if you have a family, you might not be able to move around as easily as now." Tactful as ever, Dora didn't mention the family might be Flemming's.

"Wherever you live, you might get fed up with it. Families should take root in one another's love, not in a place. Although Ærø has its troubles, it's perfect to me despite all its faults. Also, I'm striving to make it better by finding a cruel murderer. I can't stand his presence polluting the trust we islanders have in each other."

"SO ARE YOU SATISFIED, MISS DOROTEA ROSA PEPE?" said Etta, sitting in her favourite armchair in the living room, sipping a cup of hot tea in front of a burning stove.

"About what?" said Dora, waking up from her dreams of Christmas decorations, songs and presents. The hound was snoring loudly on his pillow.

"You wanted to keep Nathalie happy by finding suspects other than Sille Skytte and I'd say we've found quite a few. Now you can pick and choose as you please."

"I'm never pleased to label someone a murderer."

"Well, if we don't – and quite soon – then we may end up labelling someone else 'murdered'. If you see what I mean."

"You're right. And after all, we've gone to meet all these people with the intention of discovering the truth." Dora sighed in resignation. At times, she still found it hard coming to terms with the harsh truths of life, and she was grateful to have Etta as a tireless warrior by her side. Well, sometimes Etta would fight when there was no need to do so, but that was her nature, just as it was Dora's nature to maintain peace and reconcile arguments.

"So, let's start with Anne-Grethe and Malthe at the windmill. They didn't look like suspects to me, but then again, they had opportunity and possibly motive. Malthe mentioned the cost of living on Ærø being cheaper than the rest of Denmark, and I'm sure art doesn't pay too well."

"But his paintings and his wife's photos are really good," said Dora.

"He's no Picasso, though, so a little more money in his pockets wouldn't hurt, trust me."

"But how would he get the body into the Holms' attic?"

"I'm sure he knew Sille had her storeroom there – he mentioned having done business with her, so maybe he got hold of the keys during a visit to her shop, or he knew about Freja's study. Not the most likely hypothesis, I admit, but not impossible, either."

"But what if the Holms or Camilla had caught him going in? And with Agnieszka Kamiński, too? And how would he find the time to build the wall?"

"That's true, it would certainly be much easier for Sille or Camilla, so I believe they're on top of our suspects list. But let's keep him in mind all the same, just in case he found an ingenious way to get in. After all, the Holms were away. And whoever took the woman up to the attic, alive or dead, ran the risk of being seen."

"I wonder if the police have found any more evidence or witnesses."

"We should try to make sure our paths cross with the Chief Inspector's, which shouldn't be difficult in Ærøskøbing."

"But he asked us not to snoop around."

"We didn't snoop, we just didn't confine ourselves to our flat. We're here on holiday and we love to get to know people."

Dora wondered at this new super-social side of Etta's character, but she thought better of mentioning it.

"What about Flemming's father? That came as a bit of a surprise. He spoke to Agnieszka, do you think he might have played a role in her disappearance?"

"He might have. He's our suspect number four, though he'd have had the same difficulties as Malthe. Or maybe not." Etta got up from her armchair, spilling some tea from her cup onto poor Leon, whose rug was between her chair and the stove. Luckily, the tea wasn't hot and the hound sighed deeply, but didn't stir, knowing one of his two humans would soon dry him off. Still, how the patience of a family dog was tried sometimes.

It was a tiresome job indeed, loads of hard work for little satisfaction, so he fell asleep as Dora obligingly wiped his fur.

"You remember when Flemming and the children stopped on the road with their bikes when we were coming home. When was that? It seems as if we've been here for a lifetime."

"You mean Black Friday?"

"Yes, then. I'm sure Flemming mentioned his father lived next door to the Holms at number 47, on the second floor."

"Did he?"

"Yes, I remember Thomas mentioning our attic, and Flemming telling him he might have got it confused with his granddad's flat next door. Now, isn't it weird that everything leads back to this building?"

"It is," said Dora meditatively, patting the dog who yawned, enjoying the burning stove keeping him from catching a dreadful cold.

"In the light of this new evidence, we should move him up our suspects list from four to three," said Etta. "It'd be interesting to ask Sille if he ever used her shop. From what we know of him, it doesn't seem likely, but after all, it looks as if it was an unlikely murderer who killed the poor woman."

18

THE HOUND'S WAY

The next day, the weather was awful, wet and windy with rain pouring from the sky like stair rods. Someone up above was having fun; Etta wasn't.

By late afternoon, the rain had eased off to light drizzle. Etta didn't waste another second; she dragged Dora out of the flat and along the cobbled streets until they were in front of Sille Skytte's antiques shop.

A couple of customers were in the shop, but unlike the first time Dora had visited, Sille seemed happy to show them around, answering their questions. Etta hid away with Leon while Dora went in.

It was Tina who came to welcome her, asking if she'd had a chance to explore a little of the island and if she was enjoying her stay so far. Dora mentioned the visit to the windmill and the Gammelgaards' farm, the amazing landscape at the lighthouse, their visit to Marstal and her surprise in discovering that some of the inhabitants might not be as happy living on the island as others.

"Did you meet someone in particular who was unhappy?" the woman asked in her monotone voice.

"Well," Dora answered, wondering whether or not to give her a name, then remembering that Camilla had been completely open about her opinion, "Nathalie introduced us to Camilla Egede. I'm not sure if you know her?"

Tina shook her head, but Sille, who had finished with her customers, joined them and said, "Of course I know her. Living on the island – actually, on any island – is not for everyone. You need to have a certain type of personality. It's much easier to mind your own business in a city; there are more distractions, less time to think. On an island, you can't help but confront your true self."

She spoke with the usual impatience in her voice, then glanced at her watch. Dora feared she might be escorted from the shop at any moment so Sille could lock the doors.

"It's almost closing time, Tina, you can go," Sille said.

I figure that means I'm welcome to stay, Dora thought as Tina went to fetch her coat and all that was necessary to cope with the chilly evening. As the large woman wound a long scarf round and round her neck, Dora told Sille about Flemming's father having been spotted talking to the Polish detectorist in Marstal. The woman wasn't quick enough to hide her reaction; she went pale and her eyes opened wide as she listened to Dora's account.

"So I wondered if Villads had ever called in at your shop around that time, or if he had access to the attic keys."

"Tina, off you go, dear," Sille said to her assistant, who was almost hidden beneath her hood, scarf and mittens, waiting for the two of them to finish their conversation before wishing them a good evening.

As Tina left, Sille sat, or rather, collapsed on a chair behind her. "It's been a long day in the shop," she said by a way of an excuse.

"I'm sorry, maybe I'm tiring you with all these questions," then Dora realised that had Etta been around, she would have kicked her in the shin. It wasn't the time for courtesy; she had taken Sille by surprise, she'd have to finish the job now. "But it's very important we piece together the whole puzzle. Did Villads Grøn come to your shop at all the week Agnieszka disappeared?"

Dora's little speech had given Sille some time to recover.

"Of course not. That man was no good, and he certainly wouldn't have known anything about the value of antiques, so he had no reason to come into my shop. Now it's time for me to go home." And with that, she accompanied Dora to the door.

~

"I MUST CONFESS, I'M LOST." DORA WAS PANTING AS she tried to catch up with Etta's strides and finish telling her friend about her meeting with Sille. "Why should she react so strongly to the mention of Villads Grøn's name?"

Etta stopped all of a sudden on the tiny pavement. Leon, whose leash had gone back into Dora's hands, slammed against her legs, but Etta's brain was in overdrive. Her central nervous system, pumping all her energy into her thinking neurons, had cut off any unnecessary signals, such as pain.

"Two months!" she almost shrieked, looking right into Dora's eyes. "Villads died just two months after the Polish woman disappeared. I'm starting to smell a rat."

"You don't think..."

"I think," Etta said, agitating a menacing finger under Dora's nose, "they're hiding dark secrets on this island."

As Dora was fiddling with the keys to the front door of the Holms' house, Etta felt again the uncomfortable sensation of being observed.

"Look at the first window to our right," she whispered to Dora. The inner light was off, but the streetlamp showed a curtain was moving as if someone was spying from behind it.

"It's not the first time we've been watched since we arrived at this house. I wonder who lives there."

"It must be a cat, surely," Dora said, winking.

Etta entered the flat still feeling there was something creepy about the moving curtain. But a Christmas tree, a cosy atmosphere and a hot shower could lay even the wildest thoughts to rest. After Dora's Italian dinner made with fresh Danish ingredients, the two were reading and chatting quietly when Leon sprang up and moved to the door with a strange whimper.

"There's no way you're going to convince us to go out in this cold," said Etta, inviting him into the kitchen where there was access to the back garden. "You'll have to be happy with a quick pee, and then come straight back, preferably not too wet."

But the hound's bum didn't move an inch from the flat's door. He merely turned his head back and looked in Etta's direction with an expression that clearly said, "You humans are too thick to understand a dog's needs."

"Leon, come over here if you really need to go out," Etta insisted.

Leon changed tactic and went to sit in front of Dora with the same urgent request. But Dora justified Etta's response.

"Oh, little doggy, I promise you we'll go for a long walk tomorrow. It's too cold tonight."

Sighing, Leon went out into the small garden, made sure to water every needy plant, and came back into the house, sitting at Dora's feet. But a few minutes later, there he was at the flat's door again, this time showing a more urgent need to get out.

When both women ignored him, he launched into his trademark trio of velvety barks, "Woof, woof, WOOF", and the two hags finally understood. Leon never barked in the middle of the night, nor did he bark for the sake of barking.

"Should I take him out and see what he wants to do?" asked Dora.

"We'll go together."

Tired and unwilling, the two put their trousers and thick coats on over their pyjamas, then donned hats, scarves and gloves, Etta thanking Leon sarcastically with every garment.

"What a piece of luck to own a dog. The dear beasties really are a woman's best friend, if you're keen to catch pneumonia."

The dog didn't mind her. As soon as he was on the leash, he pulled with all his might towards the main door of the building. Dora slowly unlocked it and Leon stood with his nose in the air. Then it seemed he found the scent he wanted. Nose to the ground, he pulled, his fur bristling. Dora had to slow him down as sleet had started to fall, making the pavements slippery and dangerous for those who had only two legs.

They followed him along the backstreets of Ærøskøbing until they reached a recently vacated parking space, judging by the relatively dry patch of ground. There, Leon seemed to lose the scent.

"Probably some female dog in heat," said Etta. "I told you we should have neutered him." Leon looked at her in horror; or maybe it was only Etta's guilty conscience making her imagine he understood every word. "But in this family, whatever I suggest is never taken into consideration."

"Well, now we're out and about, let's admire Ærøskøbing when there's no one else in the street, a touch of snow on the paths, the lights at the windows... it's pure magic." Dora always had to find a positive outlook on life, especially where Leon was concerned.

"I prefer those magic few hours when there's some sunlight. Darkness lasts too long in the North for me."

"We should come back in summer and see how different the island is then," Dora suggested. Unexpectedly, Etta didn't turn the idea down. She was enjoying the vast sense of possibility that her life had taken on since she'd become close to Dora and met Leon. Nowhere was too far, even on the paltry pension the

Italian Government gifted teachers after 40+ years of work. Sharing their house meant they could save on living expenses, whilst home swapping allowed them to go where they pleased when they wanted without spending a fortune. As a pensioner, Etta was free to do what she wanted like never before.

Suddenly, there in the freezing cold of a Northern night, soaking wet as the umbrella had proved useless in the wild wind, Etta felt grateful to her two companions. But because she was Etta, she didn't mention a word of this to either of them; she just giggled inanely and didn't grumble at all on the way back home.

It took a long while to come down from the adrenaline rush of the late-night walk in the cold and return to the contented doziness of earlier. But when Etta finally took herself to bed, she drifted off in no time.

She was deep in her sleep when a weight fell onto her, waking her with a start. She was ready to cry out, but something cold and threatening reached for her neck, commanding silence.

19

INTO THE DARKNESS

My *goodness,* Etta thought. *Is that a knife or a gun at my neck? I guess I'll soon find out – God, please make it a gun. I'd rather be shot than cut into pieces. And send my blessings to Maddalena; Leon and Dora should be provided for, unless they are going to be shot or cut into pieces, too...*

The last thought was so cruel that she opened her eyes and raised her hands in defence. And those very hands found their way into the mouth... of the dog.

"Leon, what are you doing here?" Etta breathed a huge sigh of relief. "Go and get some sleep, you killer! I could have had a heart attack."

But Leon was of another mind. His front paws stayed on the side of her bed and his cold, wet nose sank even more deeply into her neck.

"Have you got a bad stomach?" Etta wondered. The dog, bless him, would never usually wake them in the middle of the night; it had only happened once when he had found a tray of lasagne with béchamel sauce. After eating it all, he suffered some harsh consequences for the next couple of nights.

Confused, Etta got up and went towards the kitchen, but Leon was pointing at the door into the communal hallway.

"No way! You're not dragging me out again. You're no longer the dog of a watchman; you're the dog of two ladies who like to sleep at night."

Leon whined and kept on pointing at the door.

"That's enough!" Etta howled angrily. There had to be some female dog in heat in the neighbourhood, hopefully not too close or their entire holiday on Ærø was going to be a pain. "Let's go back to our room, Leon," she added firmly.

"Woof, WOOF, WOOF!" was the non-compliant answer. She took hold of him under his armpits and dragged him towards her bedroom.

"Enough!"

Leon became a dead weight. He excelled at that, instantly multiplying his weight to ten times its usual 30 kilogrammes. Etta growled deeply with the effort, only to let go of the dog five seconds later when a scream rang out from the flat above. Leon squirmed into an upright position, then his long body turned into a powerful rocket that charged against the door. The long, resonating howl that accompanied his frenzy sounded like a pack of wolves had gathered in Ærø.

"Goodness!" cried Dora, emerging from her bedroom. Etta took hold of the sturdy umbrella that had been so useless during their walk and reached back to make sure Leon was OK. Dora was beside him.

"Nathalie, are you OK?" Etta cried as she opened the door, adding, "We've already called the police, they're coming," which wasn't actually true, but she hoped it would be enough to scare whoever had caused Nathalie to scream out loud.

The light on the stairs didn't come on and they climbed clumsily, Etta trying to keep the growling dog under control just in case he ran into trouble, holding the umbrella and being careful not to take a tumble. When they reached Natalie's flat, the door was wide open.

"Hellllp, there's someone in my flat! Hellllp!"

"We're here, Nathalie, and the police are coming, too..."

Leon completed the sentence with a long series of threatening barks. The two women entered the flat, Etta wondering for the first time if they had done the smartest of things, or whether they should have actually called the police and waited for them to sort things out. The lights were out in Natalie's flat, too, but guided by her cries and screams and the streetlights shining in through the windows, they made their way towards the bedroom.

It was then that they heard a tumbling noise behind them, as if someone was running down the stairs heavily.

"Nathalie, are you OK?" Etta asked again.

"Scared to death, but still alive," the young woman cried, flinging herself into Etta's arms.

"Are you hurt?"

"No, I'm not, but my goodness! I woke up and sensed that someone was in my room. At first, I thought I was dreaming, but then I realised it was a real man of flesh and bones."

"And he's cut the power off."

"There's a fuse box next to the entrance door to the flat," the young woman said, her voice still shrill. Etta went to check the fuse box in Nathalie's flat, but nothing was amiss.

"There was no power in our flat or on the stairs, either. Is there a fuse box to cover the whole building?"

"Yes, downstairs between the main door and the door to your flat."

"We need a torch," Etta said.

"I've got my mobile and there's a torch in the kitchen, but my legs feel like jelly so I'm not sure if I'll manage to walk."

Helped by Dora, Nathalie did manage to reach the kitchen and find the torch.

"Are you going downstairs all alone, Etta?" said Dora.

"The guy ran away..."

"Take Leon with you."

Etta was too scared to say something sarcastic about how ferocious and fearsome Leon was. When the two went downstairs, they found the main door open, the chilly wind blowing the sleet into the hall, but Leon, although excited, gave no sign that someone was still around.

Breathing deeply in relief, Etta found the main trip switch where Nathalie had said it would be, and her relief only intensified when light flooded the building as if it was six o'clock in the evening and not two in the morning. She closed the door, which on closer inspection didn't seem to have been forced.

On the way back up to Nathalie's flat, Leon stopped, sniffing something.

"A pipe." Etta recognised the simple item that sailors favoured in past times. She left it where it was; she'd pick it up with a napkin later.

Now that the lights were on, Nathalie had partly recovered.

"I was sleeping, so I didn't really hear anything strange, but I woke up feeling scared. I thought I'd had a bad dream, but then I felt there was another presence in the room. I remembered my flatmate Eliza is away, so I stayed still, hoping he wouldn't hurt me if all he wanted was to steal something."

"You're referring to 'he', did you actually see that the intruder was a man?"

"In the light of the streetlamp, I saw a large man wearing what could have been a raincoat. And when he came closer, I noticed a long black beard and thick eyebrows. I couldn't distinguish much else about his face, though..."

"I see." Etta pondered for a few moments. "And Leon found a pipe on the stairs. Please continue."

"When he came closer, I was afraid he might gag me, and that moment could be my last chance to raise the alarm. So I screamed with all my might and was so grateful when you shouted back that you'd called the police. As soon as he heard that, the man left my room."

"He must have lingered in the living room," Dora said, "waiting for us to come in so we wouldn't pass on the stairs."

"Can you tell if he's taken anything?" Etta asked.

Nathalie looked around, but it didn't seem as though the intruder had disturbed her things in the living room. They moved back into the bedroom, but the man didn't seem to have touched anything here, either. It was only when Etta closed the door to check what was behind it that they saw a message had been scribbled upon it in large characters:

"*Stop snooping.*"

The three women stood still in shock as if someone had slapped their faces. It had been fun speaking to people around the island, swapping theories about who could be the guilty party. Somehow, the fact the crime had been committed two years earlier had lulled them into a false sense of security, as if there couldn't possibly be any repercussions now.

"Goodness," cried Dora.

"Bad mistake on my side," murmured Etta.

"That's that, then," said Nathalie. "But when are the police going to get here? The station isn't that far."

"We haven't called them yet," Dora admitted. "All we could think about was coming to the rescue, pretending they were on their way to alarm the intruder."

"I'm going to fetch the pipe," said Etta, tearing a kitchen towel from the roll and asking Nathalie for a food bag. "Then we need to decide what to do. I suggest we all move downstairs, and you, Nathalie, sleep in our flat for tonight. Or what's left of it."

THEY WERE SITTING IN THE HOLMS' LIVING ROOM AND Dora had prepared a hot herbal infusion to soothe their nerves.

"Let's have a little chat," Etta said, "about what's just happened and what to do next. It looks like someone doesn't appreciate our sleuthing."

"I don't understand," said Dora. "Why would someone threaten Nathalie of the three of us? All she has done is accompany me to see Sille and both of us to visit Camilla, but they're women. The only man we've met is Malthe Gammelgaard, but Nathalie wasn't with us that day."

"That doesn't mean much. I believe the message is meant for the three... actually, four of us," Etta said, looking at the Basset Hound who was now snoring loudly in the middle of the room. "But if he knew Leon was in this flat, the intruder probably decided his safest course of action would be to target Nathalie."

"He kills women, but he's afraid of a Basset Hound?" Nathalie smiled incredulously.

"Most people in Castelmezzano own a little dog, and they say that a Yorkshire Terrier inside is a better deterrent than a Rottweiler outside. They're the perfect alarm system. In fact, Leon heard the intruder trying to get in earlier on, we just didn't understand what he meant..."

As if on cue, Leon woke up, yawned and turned over onto his back, his belly in the air, an invitation to cuddle him. Wasn't he the most irresistible, talented hound of all times?

"He's such a spoiled brat," said Nathalie, laughing for the first time since her earlier fright and reaching out to him while Dora told her how he'd raised the alarm earlier on, and that they'd gone outside but seen nobody.

"Maybe the man decided it would be safer to come back in the middle of the night."

"He had a key," said Etta. "He got in without forcing the door."

"That, unfortunately," said Nathalie, looking at Etta seriously, "doesn't cut down our list of suspects. It's well known where Freja Holm keeps the keys..."

"Possibly," Etta continued, "he kept them from a couple of years back, deciding they might come in handy again..."

"Should we call the police now?" asked Nathalie, looking to Etta, completely trusting her judgement.

"The Chief Inspector will be mad at us," she sighed. "When he reads the message, he will find out we've been snooping despite his warnings..."

"But," Dora cut her friend short, fearing she might come to the wrong conclusion, "if there's a killer threatening us, the police must know."

Etta looked at Nathalie, realising for the first time just how young she was.

"Call the police," she said. "That's the only sensible thing to do."

Things were as bad as Etta had feared. Chief Inspector Knudsen scolded them harshly, forbidding them to continue with their 'silly investigation' (his words) and demanding they get all the locks replaced immediately. No longer were the keys to be kept in the study; he'd ask Freja to find a safer place for the spares in the future.

Etta tried to ask Knudsen if the police investigation had led anywhere so far. The Chief Inspector frowned deeply at that question.

"That's none of your business. When we have something to share with the media, you'll be able to read it in the papers like everyone else..."

Lucas Knudsen was about to go when the shy policeman came in. He spoke to his superior in Danish, but Etta was sure she heard him mentioning Malthe Gammelgaard's name. The plastic bag containing the pipe was in Knudsen's hands; she had no doubt what he was thinking. She tried to get a few words in edgeways, but the angry Chief Inspector cut her off bluntly.

"More fool you!" she growled, retiring into her bedroom.

20

NEVER STROKE A GRUMPY CAT THE WRONG WAY

The Chief Inspector left in a flurry of threats and reproaches and whatever else he could think of to impress a sense of danger upon the three women. Later on Wednesday morning, after only a few hours' fitful sleep, Dora took Leon out for a walk while Etta asked Nathalie who lived next door.

"Next door on which side?"

"Next door on the left if you're going out. I mean the other half of this building, ground floor."

"Oh, you mean Herman."

"Who's he?"

"Nobody knows exactly. He's an old man. A couple of volunteers go to visit him every day – you know, to help him with shopping and the like. I believe a nurse and a doctor also visit him to make sure he's in good health. Why do you ask?"

"A couple of times, I have felt like someone has been observing me from that flat. I think it must be Herman, always behind a curtain, spying on us or using those stupid Ærø mirrors like they were CCTV..."

"I guess he's got nothing better to do."

"My neighbour does exactly the same, the differences being one: she doesn't use mirrors, and two: once she's spotted you, she will open her balcony door and chatter you to death."

"But she's not Danish," answered Nathalie.

"Anyway, I wonder if Herman could be our man."

"Our man?"

"The killer – the man who came here last night."

Nathalie laughed out loud. "Oh right, it's clear you've never seen him." It took a while for the young woman to contain herself and Etta gave her a dirty look. She didn't like to be laughed at, not even by Nathalie.

Under the woman's steely gaze, Nathalie regained her composure.

"Herman is tiny. He's so fragile, you'd blow him away if you were to speak too loud."

"One can always pretend to be more fragile than one really is."

"Not in his case. And remember, he's under the control of medical experts. If he were cheating, they would know."

"Is he from Ærø?"

"I think so, but I've never asked."

Etta wasn't convinced it would take much to fool the doctors and nurses. Who could really tell how strong you are? If Herman had a tendency to spy on people, there would be nothing easier than for him to take the keys from his neighbour's study. A large coat could make him look bigger, and his victim's panic would help enhance his potential threat.

"We could just speak to him," Etta ventured, not wanting to reveal her real thoughts. "Maybe he saw something last night."

"He doesn't speak to anyone."

"Is he unable to?"

"No, he speaks to the volunteers and the doctor, but it's the bare minimum. He's never replied to a greeting from me. And when he goes around the library or to do some shopping accompanied by a volunteer, he writes down the things he needs."

"Holy smoke! Isn't that reserved even for a Viking?"

"It is. And it's not that we're unfriendly, we just..."

"Don't like to speak to strangers." Etta had heard this so often since she arrived on the island, but she still took it personally when someone didn't reply to her greeting or comment, which, to be fair, didn't happen as frequently on the island as it had in Copenhagen. "Still, I wonder whether... no, actually, I believe we *must* pay him a visit."

"He will just look at us and not say a single word."

"I've faced much worse in life."

"If you say so. Let's go now before I need to leave for work."

As soon as they were in the street, Etta looked at the man's window and didn't see any movement. But Nathalie touched her arm and invited her to look straight into the inward-facing mirror placed between his window and the main door to number 47. Etta caught a glimpse of two dark, protruding round eyes, brown versions of Gollum's in the *Lord of the Rings* films.

The secret observer made Etta angry. How dare he spy on her? He'd better not refuse to speak to her after that. Not that it took much to get Etta mad at someone, but this was unacceptable by anyone's standards.

She rang the bell using her finger as if she wanted to drill a few inches into the wall. Silence. Longer ring. Some shuffling on the other side of the door. A nerve-shredding sequence of short, loud, long, angry rings.

There was a click, then the door slowly, slowly opened, one millimetre at a time. Ages later, when Etta felt her hair must have grown down below her ears, the gap was only about 20 centimetres. And from the darkness, the palest of faces seemed to materialise like ectoplasm from a medium.

Now the two large eyes Etta had spotted earlier bulged from their sockets as if they wished to escape from the skull, glaring at her from a face so stiff, hollow and pale that Etta wondered if it belonged to the living or the dead.

"I'm Concetta Natale Passolina, your neighbour, and I need to speak to you."

The man, or whatever the undead creature on the inside of the house was, stiffly moved his head in denial. As slowly as it had opened, the door started to shut.

Etta, misled by the harmless appearance of the creature, put her foot in the gap and blocked the door.

"I said that I'm your neighbour and I need to speak to you!"

With a sudden movement, as unexpected as an attack from a snake that a second before, one had thought to be a tree branch, a walking stick materialised from the darkness to hit Etta on the foot, hard. As she let out a cry of pain, the man shut the door in her face.

"Police!" Etta cried. "That man assaulted me!"

"Come on, Etta," Nathalie hushed her. "You won't convince anyone that harmless Herman hurt you."

"He could have broken my foot! In my country, that is called violence against women."

"That foot was trespassing on his private property," Nathalie reminded her. "And now I need to go to work. If I'm late, they will think twice about turning my internship into something more permanent."

As Nathalie left, Dora appeared round the corner from the Vestergade, Leon trotting beside her with the happiest smile on his face. They had gone to the bakery and the waitress had not only offered him a treat, she'd also said he was the most wonderful dog on earth. Of course, he knew that, but to have it confirmed by such a sweet young lady...

"You're never here when I need you! I've just been attacked by a violent man!"

"Oh my goodness, Etta!" cried Dora, letting go of both the

bags she was holding and Leon's leash. "What's happened? Are you badly hurt?"

"You didn't buy any eggs, did you?" Etta enquired, looking at the shopping bags lying on the ground.

"No, just bread, flour and a few cinnamon rolls. But who..."

"It was this moron next door. He hit my foot with his walking stick. I hope I don't have a fracture of the metatarsus or my little toe or..."

"You don't mean Herman, do you?"

"Exactly. Him." Etta looked up suspiciously at her friend, wondering how Dora could have known the old man's name, but she was too impatient to ask. Instead, she told Dora what had happened, spicing it up with a touch of drama in typical Etta style.

As she listened to Etta's tale, Dora recovered from her panic.

"If you really need to speak to him, I will see if he's free this afternoon."

Etta looked at her as if she had gone either deaf or mad.

"Maybe you ain't been listening to what I said. The moron won't talk to anybody..."

"So I was told, but you should never stroke a grumpy cat the wrong way. You should know."

"Sure, Miss Sugar," Etta replied touchily; she knew exactly what that innocent "you should know" meant. "You talk to him, and this afternoon he will receive us with a nice cup of tea and a spoonful of strychnine."

AT FOUR O'CLOCK, WHEN ÆRØ WAS CUDDLED UP IN the darkness of a Nordic night, when the yellow lamplight flickered on the paved roads, when the windows were lit from within, becoming pictures of domestic bliss, Dora, Etta and

Leon stood outside Herman's door. Dora, holding a container of gingerbread men, stopped Etta before she could ring the bell.

"I'll do that. Herman is rather sensitive to noise, so we'd better be as delicate as possible."

"Then we'll stay out here on the doorstep until we're frozen and will be found in the morning by some unfortunate passer-by." But Etta had hardly completed the sentence before the door started to open, slowly, slowly, one millimetre at a time. The Gollum eyes floated in the darkness as if they didn't belong to a body. Then the dim light of a few candles, maybe a lamp hidden somewhere, revealed an ancient wafer-thin man holding himself up on a walking stick that Etta knew only too well.

21

THE MIRRORS OF ÆRØSKØBING

The head nodded in a sort of greeting. Dora replied with a smile and the same nod. Etta, feeling she was entering an extraordinary out-of-this-world experience, did exactly what Dora had asked her to do.

"Don't speak, don't growl, don't slam things. Just copy me."

Easier said than done, Etta had thought, but now here she was, mimicking her friend. Even Leon seemed able to contain his natural exuberance. He stood quietly, his expression serious, wondering what was going on in this house where movement, sound and light were all muted.

Shuffling along the corridor, the man led them into his flat. Etta recognised the curtain and the window from which he would spy on them, and possibly everyone who passed by. Once they were sitting on the comfortable armchairs in the living room, once Etta's eyes had got used to the near darkness, she could finally see the man properly. Around his eyes, most unexpectedly, he had a head: a small, inquisitive head balanced atop a thin neck and the scrawniest body she'd ever seen. He was wearing pyjamas and a velvet smoking jacket, as her grandfather had once done when receiving visitors late in the afternoon. Between the pyjama bottoms and the slippers, a piece of ankle showed. Etta wondered if there was actually any flesh around it, or if it wasn't just another skeleton as bare as the one she'd found in the attic.

Without saying a single word, Dora gently opened the gift she'd prepared at home and offered a gingerbread man to Herman. His eyes twinkled. The corners of his lips, which had been pointing towards the floor so far, slowly rose to make a straight line with the middle, and didn't stop there, but continued their upward trajectory until they formed a smile. Well, at least something resembling a smile.

By the time Herman had finished munching and swallowing the head of the gingerbread man, a good 20 minutes had passed. Leon was snoring on the floor by now, while Etta felt she wanted to scream with frustration.

Dora took a little white board from the arm of her chair and wrote, "My friend and I would like to ask you a few questions."

The man read and nodded. Before Etta could ruin it all by speaking loudly, Dora rubbed out her words and passed the board to Etta, who took the black marker and wondered how she was supposed to ask everything in a single sentence. Then she remembered Nathalie telling her Danish people don't like small talk. This rule must surely apply to writing, too, so without preamble, she wrote her question.

"Apart from those who live there, did you see anyone going into our house last night?"

Herman read and nodded.

"Who?" Etta couldn't help speaking out loud, but at least she whispered so softly that the old man did not protest. Instead, he took his own board and scribbled something.

"A big man with a black beard and a long coat. He came twice: 10pm, then around 2am."

Etta, keeping her grumpy "We already knew that" to herself, wrote, "Who was he?"

The man shook his head and wrote, "I don't know."

Etta felt like a deflated balloon. She had wanted this meeting so badly, mainly because she'd thought Herman might be involved in the foul play. Now, seeing him up close, she realised that either the man had the combined acting talent of Dustin Hoffman, Meryl Streep and Robert De Niro, or he was as innocent as she. Worse, he hadn't witnessed anything of note.

Out of sheer despair, she wrote on her board, "Did you see anybody going into the Holms' house two years ago, when Agnieszka Kamiński disappeared?"

The man read and thought carefully. Then, instead of writing, he pointed his walking stick to the floor. The cane oscillated and trembled as if an elephant was using it to support himself. Herman made three attempts to stand up; the third time, he succeeded.

He moved across the room and stood in front of a large bookcase occupying the whole wall. Going through the labels of a collection of uniform grey folders, he signalled to Etta to come over. As she joined him, he pointed to a specific folder and she read the label: "Number 49", followed by the year of the murder.

She took the folder out. Inside were pages and pages of notes starting on 1 January. Etta flicked through the pages to late October and early November, the week Agnieszka had arrived on Ærø. The woman wasn't mentioned, but for every day, there was a record of the movements in and out of the Holms' house.

Etta's heart thumped with joy and expectation. Herman had recorded the time and date when the Holms had left their flat with their luggage. He'd mentioned when Camilla had gone in and out, and her flatmate, too, along with whether they were carrying shopping bags, even the shops they'd been to if the logo was recognisable. Etta scanned the pages feverishly, asking the man when she couldn't understand a Danish word in his otherwise clear writing.

Sille Skytte had gone to the attic just once, early in the week. Etta felt sure Agnieszka had been seen alive after that. Tina had gone in and out a few times, carrying what looked like large paintings. No mention of a stranger's face, an unknown woman. As far as Herman's records were concerned, Agnieszka had never walked into the Holms' building, nor had a bag large enough to hold a body been carried in.

The excitement followed by the bitter disappointment left Etta feeling more thwarted than ever.

"Any chance someone went in when you weren't watching?" she wrote.

"Unlikely, but still possible," Herman answered on his white board.

Etta resisted her overwhelming urge to expel him to hell and tell him how useless he was. The man was showing her a mirror inside the living room reflecting the mirror outside. And another one in front of the TV reflected that on the living room wall, which was reflecting the one outside. He could see what was going on in the street even when he was watching TV.

Volume off and subtitles, no doubt, Etta thought bitterly.

And he could see the main door of his own house as well as the Holms'. Years and years and years of complete records. Wasn't that better than any CCTV?

"Why?" she didn't write this, but indicated the giant bookcase whilst her lips formed the word, nothing but her breath coming out, her vocal cords dead and flat.

The man bent down to his board and wrote, "My hobby!"

After that, Dora passed him her board a couple of times to thank him for his help. The man nodded, and again the ghost of a smile appeared on his face as he wrote his answer.

Etta sneaked a look over Dora's shoulder to read, "You're welcome in any time, just remember to tell me in advance." Clearly, surprise visits were well beyond what his system could endure.

With an almost imperceptible nod, the old man called Leon. A shiver went down Etta's spine; neither she nor Dora had any power whatsoever to influence the Basset, but the dog sat up straight in front of Herman with his head tilted to one side, his brooding eyes looking straight into the man's rheumy ones. Then he raised his right paw and gently touched Herman on his knee. The man bent forward and caressed Leon's head.

Herman liked Leon, and more surprisingly, Leon liked Herman. Which, as Etta knew, meant nothing. Just as she had learned that she and Dora were unable to influence who the dog liked, she had also learnt that all the tittle-tattle that animals in general, and dogs in particular, could distinguish the good from the bad was complete balderdash. Leon, for example, had an inexplicable liking for Arturo, Dora's 'adorably talented' nephew, otherwise known as the most useless scoundrel on the whole planet. Whenever he saw the young man, Leon jumped up and wagged his tail exuberantly, something he would never do with Etta. The truth was that dogs, very much like humans, could make bad judgements of character. So the fact that Leon liked Herman meant nothing; in Etta's eyes at least, it was only the man's appearance that was testament to his innocence.

As they left the darkened house, Dora suggested walking up to the corner with the Vestergade, just to have a look at the delightful road before heading home. Etta started forward at a pace, unwilling to utter a single word. Puzzled, Dora and Leon could hardly keep up with her as she hurried all the way to the harbour. Once there, she made sure no one was around, then launched forth a powerful cry over the sea.

"What's the matter? Aren't you feeling well?" asked Dora in dismay.

"No, I've just had to keep my mouth shut for too long. I needed a little freedom." Etta breathed deeply a couple of times and massaged her gloved hands before turning to Dora with a question. “Was it true, did we really just have a silent conversation with a man using white boards?”

Dora nodded.

“And by the way, how did you manage to get us an invitation into his flat?”

Dora smiled. “We’ve been friends for a few days.”

“But he’s never shown his face outside that mausoleum he inhabits.”

“I too noticed the curtains twitching, that he looked at us bringing our shopping home, but never dared to speak. I saw him watching in the mirrors, so I knocked very softly at his window and offered him some of the rolls we had bought at the bakery. The night we went out to Flemming’s, I made a small tiramisu just for him, and he sent me a message via his nurse to thank me. So I got in the habit of conversing with him by slipping little notes through his door…”

Etta, not for the first time since her path had crossed with Dora’s post-retirement, felt utterly baffled. It would take blood, sweat and tears for her to discover something important, only to find that Dora was well ahead of her.

“Just to make things clear,” she asked brusquely to prevent any self-pity from seeping out, “do you know who killed Agnieszka?”

“Of course not, why do you ask?”

“Just want to make sure I don’t risk my life only to discover that you’ve known since before we left home.”

“How silly of you, Mrs Concetta Natale Passolina.”

“Not at all, Miss Dorotea Rosa Pepe, I’ve learned one should never take you for granted.”

She slipped her arm through Dora’s and they walked back home through the joyful Christmassy atmosphere of Ærøskøbing, their hearts bursting with feelings of friendship for each other and, of course, Mr Napoleon Basset Hound.

22

BACK TO THE ATTIC

It had been a long sleepless night. After endless hours of tossing and turning, Etta had alternately tried listening to some soft music, reading and taking a walk to the kitchen for a milky drink. She had even been tempted to go for a walk, but resisted because it was too cold. And there was always a risk that the killer suffered from insomnia, too.

Adding a generous slug of brandy to her hot milk, purely for therapeutic purposes, Etta had tried watching TV for a while. Unfortunately, the programmes were mainly in Danish, and the only German channel she could access was showing a movie about a serial killer on the loose. It featured so much blood and violence that poor Etta felt an extra-large dose of adrenaline pump into her system. This called for another cup of hot milk and brandy.

When she finally went back to bed, the pillow seemed to torture her neck, forcing it into the most uncomfortable positions. The bed linen had a tendency to twist around her body and the duvet repeatedly slipped onto the floor, while Etta was either bathed in sweat or trembling with cold. What seemed like centuries later, the time crawled round to 5 am; as she'd feared the clock had got stuck at 3 am, which made Etta feel cheated as the daytime hours in midwinter were so much shorter than the night time, that counted as good news. Along the corridor, she could hear Dora and Leon snoring from the other bedroom. Natalie's door was closed – after her terrifying experience with the intruder, the two older women had insisted she stay with them until the case was solved, so she was using Freja's study as a temporary bedroom. Etta was almost tempted to knock and ask the young woman if she fancied a little chat, but today would be a working day for her so she needed her sleep. Pesky insomnia was bound to be a solitary affair. Even the dog, usually moving between Dora and Etta's bedrooms and the living room, corridor or even the bathroom, had decided that the safest place for tonight was to stay with Dora. Etta would have given him a call, just for the company, but she guessed the stubborn hound would snore on and leave her plea unheard and ignored.

But why was she still awake? That was the pertinent question. She didn't normally suffer from insomnia; she was a sound sleeper, except when 1) she'd quarrelled with her daughter, Maddalena, 2) she had a guilty conscience or 3) she had half an idea. Not a whole idea, just half of it, and you cannot fall asleep with a partly developed thought trying to find its way out of your brain. As far as point one was concerned, the quarrel with her daughter had been ongoing since before she and Dora departed for Denmark, after Maddalena had announced she wouldn't be coming to Castelmezzano for Christmas, but Etta had been too mad at her to allow Maddalena to ruin her sleep as well as her Christmas. What about point two? Honestly? It really seemed to Etta that she hadn't behaved improperly towards anyone. Maybe it was the Christmas spirit rubbing off on her, or more likely the fact that the tough Danish folk were impervious to her blunt ways.

So it must be point three. Something was bothering her.

Their latest development had been their talk with Herman, but that didn't seem to have led her any closer to the truth. On the contrary, the much-anticipated meeting had been a real disappointment. She had gone from the high of discovering such an accurate recording system to nothing in a matter of minutes.

Her mind went back to the large bookcase, the sheer number of files, and Herman's quivering hand as it moved between numbers 49 and 47, where he lived. In fact, Herman's flat and the Holms' property were both part of a single large building that had been divided into two, and then each half further divided into flats. Had it not been for that misaligned wall in the attic, Etta would never have suspected anything. But there was no record of Agnieszka ever having entered the Holms' property at any time during her week on the island, neither alive nor dead. But she must have done. A body can't just materialise from nowhere.

If only one of the visitors to the attic had been surprised carrying a large bag. Eye witnesses had mentioned how small the Polish detectorist had been, but it would still have taken an unusually big bag to contain her body. But Herman had seen nothing of the sort.

"Unlikely, but still possible," Herman had answered when Etta asked if anyone could have passed by without him noticing. The unlikely must have happened: either the killer had carried the body in or Agnieszka had walked in at the very moment Herman was not watching. The only objects he had seen going in were a few paintings and shopping bags, and you really cannot hide a body in a picture frame, nor a couple of shopping bags, for that matter, unless the corpse had been cut into pieces. Which poor Agnieszka clearly had not.

Etta's fingers drummed on the table; she was getting agitated. She felt something was eluding her, a little detail she couldn't quite grasp. Which number, 47 or 49? Camilla Egede had lived in the first-floor flat that Nathalie now occupied,

Villads Grøn in the equivalent flat of 47, Sille Skytte renting the attic space in number 49. Herman lived on the ground floor of 47. They all orbited around her head. Again, she saw Herman's hand moving from one folder to the next. Had she been at home in Italy, she would have walked straight to his flat and rung the bell loudly and continuously until she had dragged him out of bed. But here things were different. As fragile as Herman was, if you didn't stick to his rules, he could even give Leon a few pointers on being obstinate.

No, she had to move according to his rules. She sighed heavily; cultural issues were such a bother.

Such is the irony of insomnia, as she rebelliously listed all of the things she would have done differently if she were the Almighty, sleep unexpectedly took hold of her and she was in the arms of Morpheus in no time.

~

It was a gentle rattle along the wooden floorboards of the corridor that disturbed Etta. The rattle reached her bedroom and the culprit roused her using only the power of staring.

"What's up, Leon?" she asked, putting on her glasses and peering at the hound sitting midway between the door and the bed. It was still dark, but after all, hadn't she longed for a reasonable time to get up a couple of hours earlier? She looked at her bedside clock: seven. And there were gentle noises coming from the kitchen.

"Is it Nathalie?" she asked. The dog's body wiggled positively, but he still clearly wanted her to do something. Dogs always expect their humans to know instinctively exactly what they want.

Etta got dressed and walked to the kitchen. Nathalie was indeed there.

"I hope I didn't wake you up," she whispered.

"No, it wasn't you, it was Leon. But isn't it too early for you to be getting ready for work?"

"It's Thursday, our winter bathing day. Are you sure you don't want to come along?"

"There aren't many things I'm more certain of. I don't want to dip my toe in the Mediterranean if it's not July or August; I wouldn't even consider swimming in the Baltic in December."

"You could come to watch. It's fun and we're quite a friendly bunch of people."

"I could die from hypothermia simply from watching."

"Then I'd better go, you know how I hate to be late."

"Yes, for the Vikings better a couple of days early than two minutes late."

Nathalie laughed, kissed Etta on the cheek and went to leave.

"You're irresistible," she cried, pausing at the door to grin at the older woman. Etta smiled back as a feeling of warmth took possession of her mind, body and heart. She knew she must be flushing; luckily, there was only Leon there to see. And Leon didn't care about his feisty biped's secret maternal side at all. All he was interested in was going out.

"You'll have to be happy with the garden," Etta told him.

The dog stood stoically next to the main door, as if to say, "It's either my way or none at all, even if my bladder has to burst while I wait."

"Don't bully me!" Etta retorted. "I have something I need to do, so you do your business in the garden or you'll have to wait for quite a long while."

The hound, as unhappy as he was, complied. An operation that could take him up to 15 minutes as he checked every single bush and grass blade in the garden was today accomplished at full speed. In no time at all, he was back at his post next to the front door.

Etta, in the meantime, had written a note, trying to make it as Dora-like as possible.

"May I come in for a visit ASAP? I'm very sorry for the short notice."

Then she went out, stuck the notice to the window Herman used to spy on the street and returned home to a sulky Leon. The dog felt betrayed: his human had gone out for almost a whole minute without him.

"You can come upstairs with me if you wish," she said, taking the keys to the attic, a torch and her mobile; she wanted to make sure she had everything she might need this time. Then she stopped in her tracks.

Even better…

"Doraaaaaa!"

"Yes, dear." Even after being awoken so abruptly, Dora still had a nice word for her friend. How shaming!

"I'm going up to the attic. If I'm not back in five minutes, give me a shout or call the police or do whatever you fancy."

Dora was leaning on the door frame of her bedroom.

"What's happening in the attic?"

"Nothing is happening, but that place gives me the creeps."

"Why don't you wait two minutes and we can go together?"

"I've waited all night and it won't take long and I'm sure no killer is up there waiting for me… though I'll admit, that attic still scares the wits out of me, so I want someone to know I'm there. Then, if Herman says it's OK, we can go to see him as soon as I get back. Oh, and I'm taking the dog."

"Good," said Dora, as reassured as if Leon had been Cerberus, the guard dog of Hades with his three fearsome heads. "I'll get ready."

THE ATTIC DOOR WAS STILL CORDONED OFF, BUT IF

challenged, Etta would tell the police she thought she might have dropped her precious brooch in there, a priceless jewel handed from mother to daughter for five... no, she'd make it six generations. They could arrest her if they wished.

Despite having given up its macabre secret, the room was as alarming as it had always been. Even Leon had to be dragged in with promises of a good breakfast. Etta switched on both bulbs, the one that had blown having been replaced, and stopped the door open with the heavy toolkit lying on the floor. Moving behind the bookcase, she faced the place where the police had enlarged the opening in the wall.

She pointed the torch inside the hidden chamber. The floor had been cleaned of any sign of the poor woman, but on the opposite wall, she could distinguish a patch of discolouration. It wasn't that obvious; if she hadn't been searching for it, she would never have seen it. It was as if a hole had been made in the wall, and then closed off again. And the hole would have been large enough to allow a person to drag a dead body inside the chamber. It must have been made from the other side of the building; Herman hadn't seen any DIY material being carried into the Holms' attic.

Now? Now it was time to visit Herman. Hoping he'd got the message and wasn't in a nasty mood, Etta closed and locked the attic, and she and Leon began their descent of the stairs to the ground floor.

23

WINTER BATHING

"Herman's nurse," Dora announced to Etta, who was sitting in front of her, turning a slice of bread into crumbs on her napkin, unable to eat anything for breakfast, "brought a note round from him. We can visit anytime."

"Now!" cried Etta, barely waiting long enough for Dora to put on the layers she needed to cope with Ærø's chilly air, essential even if Herman did only live next door.

A nurse opened the door to them, chatting incessantly in her sunny Central American accent the moment they crossed the threshold and laughing loudly as if she were in a normal house. Herman stood at the door of the living room, wobbly as ever on his stick but apparently not minding the behaviour of his exuberant nurse. Faithful to her promise not to break the rules, Etta scribbled a few words on her white board, asking if she could have a look at the records of number 47 for the week Agnieszka arrived on the island.

Herman gave her one of his slow smiles, the muscular effort it took for the corners of his lips to climb clear on his face. He showed her the records he jotted down daily in a notebook for the houses he... surveyed. Then at night, he transcribed all his annotations into different registers, one for each number he patrolled, so he would have ordered records to consult when required.

"And when are they required?" Etta wrote.

"Now, for example," she read from his board.

Yes, it's served me well, thought Etta, once more glancing at the bookcase full of grey folders. Herman picked out the one relating to number 47 in the year Etta was searching for and browsed through the pages. In the background, the nurse chirped on and on at Dora, seemingly without needing to draw breath.

"He's such an ordered man and keeps his records very neat. Back home in Puerto Rico, one of my aunties used to watch all her neighbours, but she never thought to write anything down..."

It was no use, Etta couldn't resist any longer. She wrote a quick note to Herman.

"How do you cope with that chatty nurse?"

Another smile spread across the old man's face, then his right hand reached for his right ear to remove an earplug for the split second necessary to show it to Etta. His face immediately impassive again, he went back to the job in hand, and when he found the relevant pages, he turned the folder towards her. Villads Grøn, at the time a resident on the first floor of number 47, just above Herman, had come and gone quite a few times, carrying not just food shopping, but also bags from a DIY store. Finally, late on the night Agnieszka was last seen, he'd dragged in a heavy suitcase, helped by a large man with a black beard.

"I knew it!" But as Etta cried out, she became aware of another fragment of the conversation between Dora and the nurse. The Porto Rican woman was telling her attentive listener that she had not gone for her usual Thursday winter swim as it had been cancelled the night before. The organiser had caught a chill from a draughty window in her office, so the winter bathing day wouldn't take place again until the next week.

"But Nathalie has gone to the pier," Etta said. "I don't think she knew it had been cancelled..."

"Then she will come back. It's not good to bathe alone, you need to have at least one partner."

"Who sent you the message?" Etta asked abruptly. The nurse told her.

At first, Etta received the news with indifference. Then suddenly, an alarm went off in her brain, as loud and intrusive as a pneumatic drill in a lunatic's hands.

"Dora!" she cried.

"What's up?" Dora asked, seeing her friend turning pale as the Christmas snow she so hoped would fall.

"We need to call the police. It all makes sense." Then she swung round to face the nurse. "Where's the winter bathing pier?" she asked. The nurse showed her the place on a map.

"Dora, you set that destination on the satnav on your mobile. I'm calling Flemming Grøn – it'd be better if he spoke to the police, just in case they waste time by asking 1,000 questions, and then telling us to stay put. We need to hurry!"

They left the nurse and Herman without an explanation, Etta gabbling a message on the phone to Flemming as she ran from the house. Leon was happy to be going for his walk finally and was getting ready to mark his scent on every tree they passed.

"No, Leon, we need to run," said Etta, ending her call to Flemming. "Nathalie's life could depend on it." Whether he understood her words or whether it was just the tone of her voice, something convinced the hound it was urgent. The lovely young woman from the upstairs flat was in danger – this only a Basset Hound of exceptional courage could deal with. He hurried alongside his humans without stopping for a single sniff. The trees would have to wait for their daily watering.

"Etta, what's going on?" Dora asked as she buckled up her seatbelt in the car.

"We've all been fooled in a most ingenious way."

"Who fooled us?"

"The only person other than Sille who could access the Holms' attic without raising suspicion and was smart enough to use the building next door for their preparations. It was from number 47 that the murderer broke through into the Holms' roof space and built the dry wall, days before they killed Agnieszka."

Dora couldn't understand much from this weird explanation. But she was too busy to ask questions; for reasons too complicated to explain, Etta could never understand what the satnav was saying, so it was necessary for Dora to translate the enigmatic directions into practical actions in real time. From Etta's urgency, though, Dora was in no doubt that the sooner they arrived at their destination, the better.

"There!" Dora cried, pointing to a tiny lane cutting through the countryside on their right. They left the car and ran past a little cottage and a few cabins to the long jetty. And at the far end, they saw a tall figure using a pole to keep a lone swimmer from getting out of the freezing water.

"Come any closer and I'll hit you on the head," the menacing figure threatened the woman in the water. "Then you'll surely drown."

Etta was wondering why she and Dora hadn't got into the habit of keeping a rolling pin in their car and how exactly they were going to subdue the figure on the pier who seemed to have taken on the dimensions, and ferocity, of a brown bear. But having no weapons, Etta would need to fight using her wits and intelligence instead.

"The game's up!" she said as coolly as if an army of a hundred soldiers was just behind her. "The police are coming and you've been found out. You'd better help Nathalie out of water or you'll be charged with one more murder."

The huge figure on the pier turned slowly towards the two women and Dora gasped as she recognised the sturdy but quiet antiques shop assistant, Tina Thorning. In her peripheral vision, Etta was keeping tabs on Nathalie, whose survival instinct had driven her back to the steps leading from the sea to the safety of the pier. Her limbs were clearly starting to seize up from the freezing cold water; she had to get out now. Even thinking about striking out for the beach was beyond the poor young woman.

Tina's face was deformed by pure hate; Etta feared she'd do something awful just out of rage and spite. If all was lost, why not get rid of the people who had found her out? Then the huge woman turned back towards Nathalie, roared with fury, and raised the pole to hit her on the head with all her strength.

Leon had never bitten anything but meat and bones before. But in a flash, he was reminded of when his mother would snap at him if he were doing something wrong. Could he do that, too? Would it violate the Canine Society's strict Code of Honour for Family Dogs that expressly forbids all canines to harm a human? But as the woman on the pier braced herself for a powerful strike, Leon saw a big, succulent bum that was just too much to resist.

It was not by any means a hard bite, but the area was sensitive enough to make sure it was a painful snap. The woman cried out in surprise, lost her balance and the pole missed its victim.

As Tina hit the water with a loud splash, Dora and Etta rushed forward to help Nathalie climb out. She was crying from the pain of the icy air on her half-frozen body. Dora accompanied the young woman to the nearest cabin in search of a blanket to warm her up, while Etta watched over Tina. The woman was grasping hold of the steps and making her way out of the sea, but it was a struggle with the water weighing down the thick coat she had donned over her swimming costume.

And that was how Flemming Grøn and the police found the scene. The Chief Inspector looked at Etta, who was holding the pole that Tina had been using to threaten Nathalie. Beside her, Leon's whole body was trembling as the hound wondered what his life would be like now that he had hurt a human.

"That's your murderer," Etta said, pointing to Tina Thorning as the woman heaved her shivering bulk on to the pier, "the one who killed Agnieszka two years ago. And she was ready to kill again to avoid punishment."

24

THE WHOLE TRUTH

News spread fast on the island. It was exceptionally rare that two cars raced out of the police station at full speed, their sirens blaring. And it wasn't long before the news became public – even if it was just unofficially, as the police hadn't yet declared that Tina Thorning had been Agnieszka Kamiński's killer.

The word spread from mouth to mouth, over the shop counters, amongst the bookshelves in the library, between the personnel at the museums, along the pavements in the cobbled streets, around the pews in Ærøskøbing church. By the afternoon, a little crowd of people had gathered in front of the Holms' house, but when Chief Inspector Lucas Knudsen arrived, they all pretended they were there by chance, just enjoying a walk. Despite it all, Etta thought as she watched the scene from her window, Vikings were not too different from ordinary people in any small town.

When Nathalie woke up in her bedroom at Etta and Dora's, she found that a few people were waiting for her in the living room. Besides Knudsen and Flemming, who was taking full advantage of the children attending after-school clubs to stay around and hear the details of the investigation, there was the surprise addition of Sille Skytte and the even more unexpected presence of Camilla, who said she had just happened to be in Ærøskøbing that afternoon. Leon was lying on his pillow near the stove; it had taken him quite a long time to get over the awful thing he had done, and he still wondered if he'd be banned by the Canine Society and refused any food. Etta and Dora had tried to convince him he had done well and the Basset for once had accepted all their cuddles, wondering if rules could be broken in rare circumstances when the stakes were high. But it was only when Nathalie, looking as pretty as ever, ignored all those present and went to hug him that he really believed the Almighty had forgiven him, or maybe hadn't even noticed the biting incident at all.

Etta helped Nathalie to take a seat in the armchair near the stove and the young woman reassured all she was definitely feeling better, although she was as tired as if she'd run a marathon. After Dora had offered everyone yet another cup of tea, the questions started. And Nathalie, with a patient smile, tried to answer every one.

She described how she had arrived at the pier that morning, noticing to her surprise that there was no one else around. Then Tina had appeared from behind a cabin, claiming she had just phoned the association's president to find out what was happening.

"She told me we seemed to be the only ones who hadn't received the message that the swim had been cancelled..."

"Of course you didn't receive that message!" Etta exclaimed angrily. "It was Tina who had sent it, and she made sure you wouldn't receive it. Later, she'd just pretend to the police that she had missed messaging your number by accident."

Tina had then suggested that since they had taken all the

trouble to get there, they might as well bathe. Nathalie had promptly agreed and got changed in the cabin. Then Tina had suggested Nathalie swim first. Nathalie had accepted without suspecting anything – for safety reasons, it made sense to take it in turns to bathe as there were only two of them.

When Nathalie had swum, Tina suggested she should stay in the water a little longer to build her stamina. When the woman had thwarted her second attempt to get out of the water, Nathalie had started to worry. Her body was aching with cold and she knew she just had to climb the steps there and then. Ignoring Tina, she had tried to do just that, only to be pushed back in the water. By this time, she was panicking, her fear compounded by Tina threatening to hit her with a pole if she didn't stay back. And that's exactly when Etta, Dora and Leon had shown up...

"I can't believe I trusted her," Sille said. "And all the time, she was a monster."

"But how did she get her hands on Agnieszka's treasure?" Camilla asked.

Etta was only too happy to take up the explanation.

"Once Agnieszka realised she had found something precious, she looked for the person most likely to be interested: Sille Skytte, the local antiques dealer. She didn't show her trove, she was just testing the waters. In fact, when Sille declared she had no interest in her treasure and that if she had really found something of value, she should inform the authorities, Agnieszka retracted her statement and said it wasn't real treasure at all, just a few buttons..."

"Yes, she also said that rather than filling in all the paperwork, she'd just leave her discovery where she'd found it," Sille Skytte confirmed. "I was a little suspicious, but on the other hand, I believed she had exaggerated its value."

"But your assistant, Tina Thorning, had overheard the conversation."

"Yes, Agnieszka and I spoke in the shop while Tina was there."

"Tina was intrigued and decided to speak to Agnieszka, reassuring her that if she really had found something valuable, she, Tina, had the right contacts to smuggle it as long as she was paid fairly. But when she saw what Agnieszka had actually discovered..." and Etta looked at Knudsen meaningfully.

"I've just come from Tina Thorning's house," the cop said. "I'm no expert, but the treasure seems to be composed of a variety of golden jewellery with amazing designs. I've never seen the like."

"Tina encouraged the woman to do some more searching," Etta continued, "assuring her she'd find a good buyer. In the meantime, she prepared the perfect hiding place. She knew she'd need a partner in crime and so she called in Villads Grøn. Villads lived in the building next door to Sille's store room, and from the unused attic above his flat, they could get access to Freja's attic. And, of course, Tina had the keys to that."

"But wouldn't someone in the building have heard them knocking the wall through?"

"Not necessarily." Looking around the confused faces in the room, Etta knew she'd need to elaborate. "Freja and Magnus were away. You and your flatmate, Camilla – I guess there were times you were out?"

The younger woman nodded. "Yes, I was doing some teaching, helping the local school with artwork, and my flatmate had a nine-to-five office job, so we were both out of the way at regular times."

"What about Herman?" asked Dora. Etta's eyes twinkled as she thought of the elderly man's secret weapon against his loquacious nurse.

"Herman has his own way of keeping out unwanted noise. I'm sure he would have employed his secret earplugs at the first sound of a commotion in the attic. And of course, he's not exactly a gossip. So that only left Villads, who was involved in the scheme."

"Why my father?" asked Flemming.

"I suspect he and Tina might have cooperated on other occasions. He had a boat and had possibly helped her to smuggle a few things from Sille's shop, or whatever she could get her hands on..."

"It would have been simpler to conceal the body directly from Freja's attic," Flemming said. "Why did she go to all the trouble of knocking a hole in the wall from the next building?"

"What better way to avoid any suspicion falling on Sille, or her shop assistant? No one ever connected the large bag being carried into number 47 with Agnieszka's death."

"Ingenious!" Knudsen said.

"They made a hole big enough for a person to climb through and built a dry wall behind the bookcase that Tina had previously pulled forward, closer to the window, when she was in the attic at number 49. And not only that, pretending she was taking some large-framed paintings to Sille's attic – what could be more normal? – she actually brought in the dry wall panels so she could finish her job on the other side of the secret room. No one ever noticed the bookcase had been pulled forward a good metre, except for the children..."

"This's why Thomas kept saying the room had shrunk," said Sille.

"Exactly! But as adults, we never really listen to what children are saying, otherwise we would have discovered the crime much earlier. So, it's the day before Agnieszka's departure and everything is ready. Tina killed her...

"The autopsy suggests a blow to her head," said Knudsen, too fascinated by Etta's account to elaborate.

"Then she put her body in a large suitcase and, with the help of Villads, carried it upstairs to the secret room they had prepared. They sealed the hole in the wall and they were done."

"But someone could have seen her taking the large bag into number 47."

"That's exactly what did happen. Our neighbour Herman recorded it, but he described a large man with a black beard helping Villads... the same *man* who threatened Nathalie on Tuesday night."

"We thought it was Malthe Gammelgaard," Knudsen said, his lips twitching into an ironic grin.

"But as soon as Nathalie told me about the black beard and wide shoulders, the bushy brows, and come on! The pipe? How convenient: the murderer leaving such an obvious clue behind for the detective. No, as soon as I heard of that thick black beard, that's exactly when I knew," and Etta pushed her large red-framed glasses up her nose because... well, she liked to emphasise how smart she had been while she had the inspector's attention, "it was a woman pretending to be a man."

"Hats off to you," murmured the Chief Inspector, looking at the sturdy little Italian woman with sincere admiration, and a bit of humour, too. "Was that what you were trying to tell me on Tuesday night?"

"Exactly!" She didn't need to add more; the victory tasted sweet enough.

"My mistake," said Knudsen. "I should have let you speak."

"But why did Tina keep working at Sille's shop?" Camilla asked. "What's the point of owning treasure if you intend to carry on with your everyday life?"

"Maybe she hadn't yet worked out her plan. Maybe she was convincing Sille to change her will..."

All eyes were on Sille.

"Of course, she knew I was going to leave everything to my grandson and granddaughter, but yes, she made a few remarks about me avoiding Flemming getting his hands on their inheritance and suggested I make her custodian of my fortune. She said she'd make sure they got their share when they were grown up, as most likely – as she put it – I'd pass before she did."

"But why did she want to kill me?" asked Nathalie.

"Because you were trying to bring peace between Flemming and Sille, whilst she was doing her best to keep the two separate, telling each a little something that'd implicate the other in Agnieszka's death."

Sille looked even more shocked. "So that was what she was up to," she said. "She told me she'd seen Agnieszka talking to Villads and passing him something, implying he was responsible without ever coming right out and saying so…"

Flemming nodded. "Yes, it was the same with me. She told me she'd seen Sille speaking to Agnieszka just before the murder. On another occasion, she said how happy she was that Sille had finally found the money necessary to buy and restore a large house overlooking the beach."

"That was money from my bank! I can account for every single krone I spent!" cried Sille indignantly.

"She was instilling doubt in each of you so you'd stay apart and there'd be no chance of a reconciliation. And that's why she was mad at Nathalie. She feared that if Nathalie married Flemming, she'd do everything in her power to reunite the family. Besides, she had seen Nathalie snooping around, mentioning Camilla, asking Sille about Agnieszka, and that's when she panicked. She could have used Villads as a scapegoat and we'd never have thought any more of it, but it seems she was blinded by the fact that Nathalie threatened to ruin all she had planned, even the nice villa she was working on making sure she'd inherit at some point. I'm sure she had more foul play in mind."

"So she created suspicions out of nothing," said Flemming.

"Well, not really out of nothing," Etta explained. "I believe Sille had some suspicions about your father, otherwise she wouldn't have been so hostile when Nathalie and Dora went to question her." Etta looked at the woman who was nervously caressing the large golden earrings she wore under her short hair.

"You're right again," Sille admitted, her eyes mischievous as she conceded the point to her former enemy. "I had seen Villads talking to Agnieszka in the pub one evening. Of course, I guessed exactly what she was offering him."

"As you never believed she had only found some simple buttons."

"Not for a moment," the woman replied in her customary blunt way, an ironic smile dawning on her face, signalling the hostilities were at an end, at least for now.

"Am I correct in thinking that, in your heart of hearts, you had always suspected Villads played a role in the disappearance of the Polish woman?"

"You knew all along?" asked Flemming, looking at Sille.

"I didn't know, I suspected. But as the police didn't seem to think anything bad had happened to Agnieszka while she was still on Ærø..."

"You wanted to protect Flemming and the children," Etta said.

Sille nodded.

"I didn't want them to have to deal with this new blow. My daughter had just died, and mad with grief, I'd stupidly tried to get custody of the children. I felt I had already done more than my fair share to make their life miserable, and when Villads drowned before the police had made sense of the whole thing..."

"...you decided to protect Villads's memory, thereby protecting Flemming and the children's feelings."

"Even when the police seemed to be suspecting you?" Flemming was stunned.

"It was the least I could do to make up for all the wrongs I've done you, Flemming."

Sille and Flemming looked at each other, unable to utter a single word, then Flemming walked over to her and hugged her.

"I knew you could be a stubborn woman," he murmured, "but you've amazed me."

Nathalie felt her heart contracting with delight. This awful story would have happy consequences after all. But to deflect everyone's attention from the reconciliation between mother- and son-in-law, she turned to Camilla.

"And how about you? I admit, we did suspect you at one point. Not only did you live below Sille's attic when Agnieszka went missing, but you also decided to move just after the body had been discovered. Why?"

Camilla flushed a little, but smiled. "I'm so happy I can tell you all the truth now. When I spoke to Agnieszka, she showed me part of her find, but only after she'd confessed to me that she wanted to leave Poland. She said she didn't want to commit a crime, but with the money she was hoping to get from selling the jewellery, she could start a better life. I told her I couldn't help her, but also that I wouldn't betray her. I know how it feels to be trapped and everyone should have a right to start again."

"Starting a new life on the back of theft?" Knudsen asked, his expression serious.

"Well, it wasn't as if she was stealing things from an individual. I knew it was wrong, but she mentioned an abusive husband at home…"

"Sure," Knudsen said, shaking his head. "An abusive husband who allowed her to go away for a week. I'm afraid she lied so you'd be more understanding."

Camilla whispered, "I was rather stupid, wasn't I? I guess I was too sympathetic…"

"So at the time, you thought she had just staged her disappearance?"

"Exactly. But when I heard her body had been found, I was shocked. I really panicked, realising that by covering for

Agnieszka, I had actually been covering up a murder. Could I turn up and confess what had happened two years before? Especially as her body had been found one floor above my former home." She looked apologetically at Knudsen. "I was really afraid the police would believe I was a suspect. I was so agitated, I didn't sleep a wink on Saturday night, then on Sunday morning, I decided it was time I made my dream come true and left the island once and for all..."

"You started to pack on Sunday and planned to rent a storage unit on Monday and buy your ticket to Copenhagen," stated Etta.

"That's correct. How did you know?"

"You had it all written in your organiser. I thought it was a strange coincidence that someone who said she'd started planning to go weeks earlier would leave it so long before enquiring about storage unit prices."

Camilla blushed. "No coincidence, just a direct consequence of your discovery. But maybe there's another good thing to come out of it: Agnieszka's untimely death has finally taught me not to procrastinate and waste any more of my time. I need to live my life as I want now."

"Was my father really involved in all this?" Flemming seemed to be just as hurt as Sille had feared.

This man, thought Etta, *is OK when he's organising big projects to save the planet and environment. He's a good educator, an excellent father, but he badly needs a wife to help him deal with the nitty gritty of life.*

"Frankly," she said, "I don't think your father had anything to do with the murder."

"*What?*" said Knudsen.

"You believe my father *wasn't* involved in the murder?" Flemming asked incredulously.

"Absolutely sure," said Etta. Actually, she wasn't as sure as she pretended, but some variations on the truth are better told with great conviction. "Otherwise he wouldn't have agreed to hide the body so close to his flat; as a sailor, he would have suggested throwing it into the sea. A heavy weight in the case and they'd be done with it. I'm sure it was Tina who murdered Agnieszka, and that she was alone when she dragged the body out of the bag and hid it in the secret chamber."

"But Herman," Knudsen protested, "told us – actually, told you – he saw the two of them carrying the luggage into next door."

"That's true, but in all likelihood, Villads Grøn was convinced the bag contained the treasure and it had to be kept hidden while the police conducted their investigations. But after a couple of months, Flemming, your father must have asked about the treasure. After all, as far as he knew, they'd hidden it to avoid raising suspicion, but now it was time to cash in. But Tina, of course, wasn't disposed to share her hoard with anyone. Or maybe your father put her reticence together with Agnieszka's disappearance and started to suspect something; maybe he even asked Tina what had happened to the woman. It was then that Tina decided she had to get rid of him."

Knudsen, a wry grin on his handsome face, looked sceptically at her, but decided to go along with her theory; Sille, unseen by Flemming, gave Etta a thumbs up; Dora squeezed her arm; Leon wagged his tail, hoping now the explanations were over, it'd be time for some serious food.

But for poor, wretched Flemming, the shocks weren't over yet.

FLEMMING AND SILLE HAD BEEN TO FETCH THE children from their after-school clubs, the delight on the two young faces at seeing their father and grandmother reconciled a joy to behold as they burst into Etta and Dora's flat in a cacophony of excited chatter. But Nathalie, as much as she loved the company, was still feeling weak, and after a while she announced she'd go back to her room for a sound sleep. They all wished her goodnight, but when Dora offered to accompany her to her bedroom – the young woman would stay with them for a couple more days until her flatmate was back – Etta kicked her friend on the shin, hard.

"No, actually, I won't accompany you," Dora corrected herself, rubbing her bruised leg and casting a rueful look Etta's way.

"Yes," Etta smiled a large false smile in reply, "we still have a few more things to go over. Flemming, dear, would you mind accompanying Nathalie and making sure she's got her hot water bottle and some tea?"

The man looked immediately apprehensive.

"Maybe it's getting a little too late and the children have school tomorrow…"

Thomas and Emma silenced him with a reproachful glance.

"Dad," said Thomas in all seriousness, "I promise we will be up early tomorrow. If we get a little less sleep than usual for one night, it won't hurt us dreadfully. After all, we almost always pretend to be sleeping when you tuck us in, but then we get up to read or play for much longer."

"And I often come to put a blanket over you when you fall asleep in front of the TV," Emma added. "And close your mouth when you snore too hard."

"This man desperately needs someone to take care of him!" Etta cried, as if shocked at the children's revelations, winking at them behind their father's back. The children nodded, their faces straight.

Flemming's face was ablaze. "I'll speak to you later," he muttered to his children with narrowed eyes, then, resigned to his fate, he went into the kitchen for the teapot and hot water bottle Dora had prepared minutes before.

When he entered the bedroom, Nathalie was sitting up in bed, her back against the pillows.

"What an honour!" She smiled at him. He remained silent and poured some tea into a cup, adding a spoonful of honey from the tray Dora had prepared and handing it to Nathalie. Only when she had taken a sip did he speak.

"How are you feeling?"

"I'm fine, really, just a little weak." She paused, looking at him with a wicked smile, patting the bed beside her, inviting him to sit. "Wouldn't it be good if you were next to me every night and we could ask each other how our day had gone?"

"Nathalie, let's not go into this again. You're lovely, but you're so very young; you'd only regret it later. And your love would turn into resentment against me for having deprived you of your carefree years."

Flemming was partly right, they had talked about this before, and usually Nathalie would plead with him for a while, and then resign herself to the strength of his reasoning, the sense of his logic. But today she had faced death, so she went off like a coiled snake.

"You're such an impossible man! And you're a coward, too." She raised herself from her bed, despite his protests to stay put. "You've decided you can only live in the past, haven't you? But I have a revelation: you're 35, not 99; are you going to live like a monk for the rest of your life? Do you think your wife would be happy if she knew you were determined to beat yourself up? If it had been the other way round, if you had died instead of her, is this what you'd wish for her? Never to marry again? Deprive your children of a father figure, even if she were to meet the right man?"

Flemming looked shocked at her reaction. Strong feelings, spoken so forcefully – this was not what he was used to. He'd never known Nathalie had so much passion inside.

"Do you think I want to take their mother's place in your

children's eyes? No! I don't want that, at all. Did I plan any of this? Was I searching for a widower with a couple of children? Nope. I'd never cared for children until I met Thomas and Emma, and then I fell in love with them. And guess what? They love me back. It's happened, you can't deny nor change it. And in the same way, you can't deny I've loved you from the first moment I laid eyes on you."

This didn't have the tone of a romantic declaration at all. Nathalie was furious and she was shouting, and it didn't bother her at all if the others were listening from the living room. She was frenzied, unstoppable, on a roll.

For his part, big, strong Flemming had dwindled down into a cowering wreck. He was so taken aback, he shrank into the corner of Nathalie's bed. All her shock and tiredness forgotten, her blood pumping, she stood up, towering over him. Her rage was so out of control that she took one of the pillows and hurled it to the floor.

"You're so damn stubborn, I don't know what to do with you!" More pillows flew in the air. "Why you, of all the reasonable men I could have met on the island?" When she turned to face him, her eyes were on fire. She gripped his head and forced it up so she could look into his eyes. Flemming wondered if she was going to slap his face, or even cut his throat. Then she kissed him. And she kissed him and kissed him until she felt the ice around his heart melt, until she knew he loved her just as much as she loved him. Only then did she let him go.

He sat still, his body trembling slightly, his eyes wide open in shock.

"Nathalie, what have you just done?"

"I've just taught you a lesson, Mr Grøn!"

A smile brighter than the Northern Lights appeared on the man's face.

"It would seem I'm a very slow learner," he said. "Maybe, I need more instruction..."

And Etta, Dora and Flemming's children, unashamedly peering through the doorway in an act of espionage that the old master spy Herman would have been proud of, silently high-fived each other, their eyes gleaming with joy.

LOST AND FOUND – EPILOGUE

It was 13 December, the Feast of Santa Lucia. Etta and Dora were due to leave the island in a couple of days and their friends had decided not simply to have a *Julefrokosit* dinner with them – one of the many long lunches or dinners Danish people enjoy with their friends and colleagues to celebrate Christmas, starting six weeks before the holiday itself. Since the two women would be gone soon, they'd decided to celebrate with presents and food as if it was Christmas Eve. Emma and Thomas were beside themselves with joy: it looked as if they'd get two Christmases this year. Leon wondered what all the fuss was about, but he hoped there would be some nice food coming his way.

That afternoon, all the citizens of Ærøskøbing had been invited to see the Vikings' treasure, found in Tina Thorning's flat, which was now on display at the Ærø Museum where it would stay until the Christmas season ended. Then it would go to Copenhagen for restoration and cataloguing before being returned to the island. Etta, Dora and Leon were publicly thanked for their part in solving the mystery and returning the trove. But the excitement of the day had only just begun.

In the evening, a procession of young girls swept along Ærøskøbing's streets. They were each dressed in white with a red ribbon at their waist, a leafy green garland on their head, a candle in their hands. The youngest one wore a crown of candles on her long blonde hair as they all sang the traditional *Santa Lucia* tune while they marched towards the harbour.

"Bringing light into the darkness," Dora said, her hands clasped, her eyes a bit watery, prey as she always was to emotions that made her life, as Etta would say, at least three times more intense and sentimental than most people's.

When the procession was over, Emma slid her hand into Dora's.

"And now we're going to Grandma's, and Dad's coming too."

Sille Skytte had wanted them all at her home for the classic Christmas dinner, and of course, no one had dared to oppose her. Although in all truth, this time, no one had wanted to. In typical Danish style, there were no huge, ostentatious decorations in her garden and porch; just simple pine cones at the windows and a huge Christmas tree in her living room. The real candles on the tree were lit as soon as the guests came into the house. The table was a triumph of white. In the middle was a large bowl filled with water, green leaves at the bottom and white candles floating amongst red rosehips on the surface. Small green garlands sealed each napkin, and a few white model reindeer were scattered on the table amongst more pinecones and candles. Looking across the table to the balcony, they could see the garden, and the sea glittering in the moonlight beyond the path where Dora, Etta and Leon had walked during their early days on the island. Fleming kissed Nathalie under the myrtle wreath and blushed as his children, soon followed by all the other guests, clapped their hands.

Sille had made a delicious traditional meal of roast duck stuffed with apples and prunes, caramelised potatoes and pickled red cabbage. And to the delight of both children and adults, *æbleskiver* – round puffy pancakes fried in a special pan – and *risalamande* – the traditional Danish rice pudding – appeared for dessert. Finally, they were invited to help themselves to a selection of freshly baked biscuits such as vanilla wreaths, St Lucia saffron buns and Danish *pebernødder* that Sille had hung in decorative paper cones on the Christmas tree.

At long last, it was time for the Danes to exchange presents with the Italian guests. Leon received the most, and what a delight it was to see his excitement and how expertly he tore the paper from them, holding each gift with his paws and using his mouth to rip the wrapping away. He didn't much appreciate the reindeer ears he'd received, and it got even worse when he was asked to wear them for a photo. Why do humans do such stupid things? At least they acknowledged that he looked so very charming. But what really improved his mood were the edible goodies. They were simply fantastic, even if Etta did tell him he could not eat them all at once.

Dora got a Danish recipe book, a charming tin filled with all the spices used in the recipes and a collection of soaps handmade in Ærø. Then Etta handed her a box. Inside, she found a snow globe containing a bridge enclosed by Gothic towers.

"But this has nothing to do with Denmark," she said, puzzled.

"And here's the other half of the present," said Etta, handing her the printout of an email.

"An invitation for a home swap!" Dora cried excitedly. "Prague! Prague for the spring? Do you really think we could say yes to this?"

"The house doesn't look bad, and it's really close to the Charles Bridge..."

From that moment onwards, both Etta and Leon knew Dora had left Ærø. She was flying over the Vltava River, the dreamy spires and the red roofs of the most romantic European city.

As for Etta, she opened her gifts to find a woollen scarf that Nathalie had knitted for her and a silver bell, from Sille, so she could keep people silent when she spoke. Then, because Etta had found the almond in her *risalamande,* an extra gift was handed to her. It came in a colourful box, and all eyes were glued on her as she opened it.

There was a letter inside. "To Mum" was handwritten on the envelope. Etta didn't want to open it in front of an audience, but soon realised she had no choice as they were all waiting. Sighing, she cleared her throat and read in a tone far quieter than her usual way of speaking.

"Dear Mum,

I'm very sorry, you were right. There's nowhere we'd rather spend our Christmas than back home, so we're coming to Castelmezzano after all. We can go skiing any time of year, but there's only one place for Christmas.

With love.

Maddalena (who's got a talent for driving you mad)*

** Not that it takes that much to drive you mad*

*** Just a stupid joke.*

**** I love you!"*

There were cheers and claps from the guests and WOOFs from Leon, who could never resist joining in when people were clapping their hands. Etta left the table and went closer to the Christmas tree, pretending to look outside as her eyes had gone a little watery. It was that rice pudding. A tad too sweet for her liking, it tickled her throat…

She cast a threatening look over her shoulder to Dora, but her friend smiled back benignly. Dora must have got in touch with that daughter of Etta's and convinced Maddalena to come home for Christmas. But as hard as she tried, she couldn't be mad at Dora for doing so. After all, now she had her Christmas back, and she wasn't the only one.

Yes, this Christmas was all about losing and finding. A woman had tragically lost her life, but the treasure, itself lost for so many centuries, was back with the descendants of the people who'd forged it. The Grøn children had their grandmother back. Flemming had found in his mother-in-law a woman who might be a pain, but had been determined not to ruin his memories of his father. And he had found a girlfriend, too: a young woman who loved him and his family dearly. Camilla had found the courage to live her life as she wanted. Even Anne-Grethe and Malthe Gammelgaard had found that allowing people into their lives was not necessarily an evil.

Etta was still deep in thought when she sensed a presence behind her.

"You'll have to come back," Nathalie whispered.

"And you can come to visit us in Castelmezzano."

"I'd love that, and so would the children… all three children, I mean," she added, pointing to Flemming.

"And Dora keeps repeating how much she wants to see the island in the summer season."

"In the meantime, I will miss you sooo much," said Nathalie, hugging her. Etta was taken aback. In such moments, she never knew what to say, so she went for something as inconsequential as she could.

"You're not being very Danish!"

"On the contrary, I'm being perfectly Danish."

"Vikings do not befriend people that easily."

"That's because for us, there's no such thing as a momentary acquaintance. Once a Viking befriends you, their friendship is forever."

I really hope you enjoyed this book. **Is there any way a reader may help an author? Yes! Please leave a review on Amazon, Goodreads and/or Bookbub.** It doesn't matter how long or short; even a single sentence could say it all. We might be in a digital era, but **this old world of ours still revolves around word of mouth**. A review allows a book to leave the shadow of the unknown and introduces it to other passionate readers.

Grazie :)

MORE BOOKS FROM ADRIANA LICIO

THE HOMESWAPPERS SERIES

0 - Castelmezzano, The Witch Is Dead – Prequel to the series

1 - The Watchman of Rothenburg Dies: A German Travel Mystery

2 - A Wedding and A Funeral in Mecklenburg : A German Cozy Mystery

3 - An Aero Island Christmas Mystery: A Danish Cozy Mystery

4 – ***Prague, A Secret From The Past*** – coming in Spring 2021

AN ITALIAN VILLAGE MYSTERY SERIES

0 - And Then There Were Bones. The prequel to the *An Italian Village Mystery* series is **available for free by signing up to www.adrianalicio.com/murderclub**

1 - Murder on the Road Returning to her quaint hometown in Italy following the collapse of her engagement, feisty travel writer Giò Brando just wants some peace and quiet. Instead, she finds herself a suspect in a brutal murder.

2 A Fair Time for Death is a mystery set during the Autumn Chestnut Fair in Trecchina, a mountain village near Maratea, involving a perfume with a split personality, a disappearing corpse, a disturbing secret from the past and a mischievous goat.

3 - A Mystery Before Christmas A haunting Christmas song from a faraway land. A child with striking green eyes. A man with no past. A heartwarming mystery for those who want to breathe in the delicious scents and flavours of a Mediterranean December.

4 - Peril at the Pellicano Hotel – A group of wordsmiths, a remote hotel. Outside, the winds howl and the seas rage. But the real danger lurks within.

More books to come in Summer 2021

ALSO

"When The Clock Chimes Two" a short story in ***"Mystery Follows Her"*** a collection of intriguing and light-hearted stories by nine award-winning and best-selling authors from across the globe. My own story features Giò Brando, Agnese and a mischievous perfume with a mesmerising name "Passage d'Enfer". It can be a good introduction to the ***An Italian Village Mystery*** series.

"Life Lines" a three-page story featuring Giò Brando and her Grandmother in **"Stop the World: Snapshot From a Pandemic"** 40 authors from around the world set out to record their innermost feelings -- to offer inspiring, heartfelt, creative takes on the Covid-19 pandemic. Crime fiction, elegant and angry poetry, and gut-wrenching personal essays: all paint a picture of the year and help us make sense of the sacrifices we've made in 2020.

AUTHOR'S NOTE

On the road

I can't exactly remember how my hand, drawing an ideal route from one homeswap in Sweden to the next in Amsterdam, stopped midway and refused any rational choice for a night stop. Copenhagen? Odense? Somewhere on Jutland close to the E45? No, it ventured a little further south to the weirdest triangle of an island which had a simple if unfamiliar name: Ærø.

It wasn't by any means the straightest route. Nor was it the easiest. As it is an island in the Baltic Sea, we would need to take a couple of ferry rides to come and go from Ærø. Not a long crossing by any means, but still – on an already long journey, you don't want to add a round ferry trip of 150 minutes if you can help it.

My hand went back to the sensible route, but when I switched on my mobile, it wasn't to check Google Maps, but to look up Ærø Island and see what Google came up with. Most annoyingly for the other two passengers in the car, namely my husband and my dog, what I saw enchanted me immediately and irremediably. A little island of quaint fishing villages, pretty white churches, coastal paths, traditional windmills, a white castle with a fascinating drawbridge and, of course, a romantic lighthouse. What more could you ask from a single place barely the size of Copenhagen city (88km^2) and a tiny fraction of the Copenhagen metropolitan area (2,778km^2).

The little streets of Ærøskøbing, its old houses, its harbours – they were all tantalising, even on the small screen of my mobile, but I confess I fell in love with the way the visitor reviews, the tourist bureau itself and the businesses of the island presented its many activities, products and services, describing Ærø as the Island of Happiness. And then there was the sheer variety of things they mentioned: organic farmers producing honey, juices, marmalades and wines, permaculture, sustainable energy independence, young people working as a team to help those wishing to relocate to the island and change their lives, weddings – because who can resist the temptation to celebrate their favourite day surrounded by beauty? – and bakeries I cannot bear to think of on an empty stomach…

Minutes later, I was phoning our Amsterdam homeswapper partner and asking her if it'd be a problem if we were to arrive two days late. Back home, I had planned a single overnight stop between Sweden and Holland, but now I decided that any fewer than three nights on the island would be an injustice.

The homeswapper partner sighed and said that of course it was to be expected, we were Italians after all and it wasn't our fault if we were unreliable when it came to timing. I felt outraged, not because it was untrue, but because it's one thing if *I* say it, another kettle of fish if *you* say it. Just before I blasted her for her slander, I heard a chuckle from the other end of the phone.

"Just a joke! Where are you going, beautiful?"

Still a little resentful – was that an example of Dutch humour? – I mentioned Ærø, and it being midway on our journey.

"Midway? Sure!" she said sarcastically. "But it's such a

charming place, you won't regret it. After all, you can always come back to Amsterdam, but Ærø is a bird of another feather! Enjoy it, love it and say hello from me."

We were in Svendborg when we met the first pirates – I beg your pardon, sailors. They were having lots of fun on the weekend, sitting at a large table amongst the ships as if they were in a cottage garden, laughing and cheering. The sun was slowly setting and they were enjoying plenty of food – Frodo, my canine companion, can vouch for the quality of what they were eating. And already, I loved these people.

Then we were on our ferry. The crossing, the sea air, the temperature so pleasant even for a Mediterranean, and best of all, I had a whole 75 minutes to dream the dream...

No treasure (yet!) found on Ærø

There has never been treasure discovered on Ærø, and frankly, the island, a treasure in itself, doesn't really need it. But what a temptation treasure offers to writers and their cast of characters. When, during our visit, we walked to the Søby windmill, we found the clues from a treasure hunt organised for children. And I simply couldn't get what a perfect spot it'd be to find some Viking gems off my mind. After all, Viking troves are common in Denmark, and as the Ærøskøbing Museum director mentions in the novel, real Viking treasure was found on the island of Hjarnø (in truth, this was in 2018 and our adventure takes place a few years earlier, but we authors are free to move minor events when and where we please). Do Google the island name to see the refined precious jewels that made up the trove. They're simply enchanting.

Certainly, Ærø has custody of quite a few treasures: its traditions, its landmarks, the beauty omnipresent on the island, and mostly, its people.

The issue with Danish Cosies

At first, I was exhilarated with my idea, and then came the results of my research. My goodness! There were quite a few cosies set in Denmark. I was hitting a popular genre. My ability to follow the market had finally improved and I would become a millionaire author! I had found a niche that was populated, but not overwhelmingly so. Readers loved cosies set in Denmark, but there weren't so many that I'd never be found.

On closer inspection, I made three discoveries. One, not all cosies with the word "Danish" in the title have anything to do with Denmark. Two, Danish is the English name for a pastry. Three, as hard as it was to believe, I was to find one and only one Cosy Mystery set in Denmark, *Death Comes to Strandvig* by Diane Hansen, who is a Scottish author married to a Dane and has lived there forever.

When I'd recovered from the loss of royalties showering me rich, I started reading. I confess, I got the chilling idea of winter bathing from Diane's mystery. How can I explain how shocking it seems to a Mediterranean that anyone in their right mind might indulge in such a torturous habit?

If you want to know more about Denmark, please read Diane's book, which is a bit different from other cosies I've read. It will immerse you, quite literally, in the country's culture. There's only one book in the series at the moment, but when called back to her duty by this hungry Cosy reader, she promised she'd publish more. Also, Diane runs a successful YouTube channel, very useful (and fun) if you want to learn more about Danish food and traditions. Just search for Diane in Denmark.

I have a feeling the Danes love their Nordic Noirs better than Cosies (or maybe they don't know what they're missing). There are plenty in the Noir genre by famous Scandinavian authors (Viveca Sten, Camilla Läckberg, Stieg Larsson, Henning Mankell to name a few). By Danish authors, there's *The Boy in the Suitcase*, the first book in the Nina Borg series by Agnete Friis and Lene Kaaberbøl. Compelling writing with a dedicated and deeply human main character, it covers gritty subjects such as violence against women, child trafficking, enslaved refugees – it's the type of book I feel I need to read, but I'll take months to recover from it. This might not be the case for you, of course; I'm not the bravest of women, I know.

Travel books

My fascination for travel books is skewed towards a peculiar niche: those about people who move, even for as short a time as a year, to a new place to experience a totally different culture from theirs. In no other book can you read (and enjoy) the culture clashes; the things that make one place so different from another. When you read books written by a local, you're immersed in their normality, their ordinary life. But foreigners moving in are like alarm bells, highlighting every single idiosyncrasy that a local simply might not be aware of.

I plunged into the pages of *The Year of Living Danishly* by Helen Russell and enjoyed all her research and thoughts, and her moments of despair. From a hectic life in London, on a cold January day, she, her husband and dog landed in an unknown and almost deserted village in Jutland. Not that the inhabitants had disappeared, there hadn't been an alien invasion; they simply *hygged* inside the comfort of their homes for the next two months, leaving the poor just-landed foreigners alone.

Still, Helen maintains Denmark is the happiest land on the planet, and she goes on to investigate the hundreds of shades Danish happiness can take.

***We the Drowned* by Carsten Jensen**

This is the only book I've found – although I only checked the ones translated into English – set on the Island of Ærø. Well, that's not entirely true as the book isn't confined to the island. On the contrary, it spans the stories of generations of islanders exploring oceans and seas around the world, as it describes the lives of Marstal sailors. Make sure to read it before you visit Ærø, then you'll have the same fun as Dora, matching real places and things to what you've read in the book.

A Christmas book

Finally, after rereading the manuscript, I'm concerned that some readers may find it a bit sentimental for a mystery. The thing is that a Christmas mystery is bound to be unlike one set at any other time of year. In brief, I absolve myself of any responsibility. Blame it all on the Christmas spirit.

PS to you

If you happen to find a Cosy Mystery set anywhere in Denmark – check it's not an American bakery cooking Danish pastries – then please let me know.

ABOUT THE AUTHOR

Adriana Licio lives in the Apennine Mountains in southern Italy, not far from Maratea, the seaside setting for her first cosy series, ***An Italian Village Mystery***.

She loves loads of things: travelling, reading, walking, good food, small villages, and homeswapping. A long time ago, she spent six years falling in love with Scotland, and she has never recovered. She now runs her family perfumery, and between a dark patchouli and a musky rose, she devours cosy mysteries.

She resisted writing as long as she could, fearing she might get carried away by her fertile imagination. But one day, she found an alluring blank page and the words flowed in the weird English she'd learned in Glasgow.

Adriana finds peace for her restless, enthusiastic soul by walking in nature with her adventurous golden retriever Frodo and her hubby Giovanni.

Do you want to know more?

Join the **Maratea Murder Club**

You can also stay in touch on:

www.adrianalicio.com

<<<<>>>>

facebook.com/adrianalicio.mystery
twitter.com/adrianalici
amazon.com/author/adrianalicio
bookbub.com/authors/adriana-licio

Printed in Great Britain
by Amazon

12718963R00120